The Cook

Also by Wayne Macauley

Blueprints for a Barbed-Wire Canoe
Caravan Story
Other Stories

The Cook

WAYNE MACAULEY

Quercus

First published in Australia in 2011 by The Text Publishing Co
First published in Great Britain in 2012 by

Quercus
55 Baker Street
7th Floor, South Block
London
W1U 8EW

A CIP catalogue record for this book is available
from the British Library

ISBN 978 1 78087 637 5

10 9 8 7 6 5 4 3 2 1

Printed and bound in Great Britain by Clays Ltd, St Ives plc

For Arch

My God, I do hope I shall make something of myself one day...
– Robert Walser, *Jakob Von Gunten*

So here I am and no going back. There are sixteen of us all stupid kids from shitkicking suburbs we all sleep in the shearers' shed. It's an old building but they've fixed it up. I am on the top bunk Hunter is on the bottom Hunter is from Coolaroo he likes death metal and wants to be a traffic controller but now he is going to be a chef like me. I won't tell you what he done I don't think it's right to tell you what everybody done I won't tell you what I done either. A year below me just turned seventeen most of us are sixteen or seventeen I think I'm the oldest here.

Cook School is a nice place but that doesn't mean it's a holiday if that's what you're thinking we get up at six! An hour and a half in the minibus from Melbourne. On that first Sunday they showed us around. It is very big the land I mean there are sheep and cows and pigs and chickens we'll learn to kill and cook them all a big vegetable garden too which is organic that means they don't put chemicals on it. There is every kind of vegetable and herb there you should see it. There are fruit trees too maybe twenty different kinds.

The Assistant Chef's name is Fabian he's the one that took us around. A red nose and pox scars on his cheeks. He says we won't see Head Chef who I'm already scared of till he comes up next week. Don't be scared Fabian says he hasn't killed anyone yet. Head Chef is famous in the business and has done pretty well for himself even though he is from a crappy suburb like me. He's the one with the telly show. Someone's phone rang give it here Fabian said. Everyone had to hand in their phones then he didn't say when we'd get them back.

After that the walk around I mean Fabian said we could have some free time before dinner. I didn't know what to do I had no friends yet I walked up the hill at the back of the property there's a cow track there that zigzags up to a tree about halfway up a fat old gum the bark all rubbed the ground trampled and dry a fallen log for a seat. I stopped and looked around. It's a pretty place. The main house down there a big old homestead a tree an oak I think in the yard the bunkhouse the new kitchen building raw timber and thin corrugated iron in front of that the vegetable garden the chookpen the fishtanks gravel paths the sun going down a hot summer's day the little insects out and right across the valley into the distance the air all mellow and gold and gold flashes coming off the windscreens of the cars way out on the highway. I could hear voices talking too but low no-one had yelled yet everyone was stepping lightly and from the big shed over the other side of the hill a piece of machinery an angle grinder I think. It felt strange all right leaving home like that but no regrets what I done coming here was a good thing what else was I going to do? That was the wrong crowd they were right.

I spent a long time up on the hill no-one came up looking eventually I heard Fabian calling out for dinner and saw everyone down below. But before I went down I had a picture in my mind let me tell you about it of a restaurant my own restaurant very modern somewhere down by the docks and Mum and Dad and my sister Tash are my special guests at my best table and Mum I kiss her cheek and Dad I shake his hand and when I show my sister Tash her seat I pull it out like the movies and she says thank you Zac and when I snap my fingers the waiters do what I tell them bring that plate yes Chef no take it back another one now a clean one please. So there's a dream who knows if it will come true but that's the dream I had that day when I went back down the hill.

Monday our first proper day and Fabian the Sous Chef that means Assistant Chef showed us around the kitchen which like everything else here is big. There is a knife for everything not like at home where one will do we have to learn about them all. Also the pots I have never seen so many pots. And frying pans. Fabian made a pasta bang bang bang you should see how fast he goes! When he finished he handed it around we each had a taste it was nice but a bit spicy for me. Some of the kids held their forks with a fist you could see Fabian's face but he didn't say anything because it's early days and we're still learning those kids will get it eventually.

Next he showed us the coolroom you walk right in there are meat hooks and shelves a pallet jack it's very cold don't get locked in Fabian said then the storeroom that's for dry goods and last a little office a table a chair a few recipe books a computer for writing home. To finish that day Fabian gave us a carrot to chop well you've never seen anything so funny in all your life some people had never chopped a vegetable before I reckon some of them had never even seen one. At the end Fabian said well that's good people we don't want to peak too early and everyone even me laughed.

The dining room I haven't told you about the dining

room we all have dinner in there it's just off the kitchen at the far end it reminds me of that camp I went to in primary school and me that night in the girls' dorm when they asked what I was doing I said borrowing a cup of sugar Mr Stirling whacked me for that. Two long tables a servery in the wall a weedy-looking guy called Gary cooks but here's the thing. We're all learning how to do restaurant food top-class top-shelf but what this Gary guy serves well to call it food is an insult to food maybe slops but even that's a compliment. That first night a sort of casserole or stew with beans and mashed potato. Fabian stood up and welcomed us all to Cook School and talked about all the great dishes we would make how funny was that I mean with those slops lying there in front of us like that. Hunter said maybe they're showing us bad food so we can see the difference between the two but I don't know looking around I don't think half of them cared.

Let me tell you about Hunter. Rough on the outside soft on the inside straight blond hair shoulder-length he left school early got in trouble yes sir no sir the judge waving his finger just like he did with me. At first we didn't make friends I didn't really want to make friends yes I know but when you're sharing a bunk with someone you get to know them pretty quick he's got a good sense of humour too. When Fabian said *al dente* Hunter said like a dentist and everybody laughed. I think it's good to be a bit of a joker but not too much Hunter wants to get somewhere I reckon he's ambitious but maybe not as much as me.

Those first few days went pretty quick the weather warm the bed OK I wrote one email home. Me and Hunter sat together most days breakfast lunch and dinner at the tables outside the dining room under the pergola or when it was hot on the grass under the trees in the orchard. We talked a lot about what we both done what our judges said how we got selected what we wanted next. It was good to talk to someone not myself. I told him how I told my mum and dad before I left I was not going to be a loser anymore I was going to change and Hunna said funny he said that too. We got pretty close after that.

Wednesday three kids dropped out there are only thirteen now all boys no girls girls don't make good chefs. They're good people mostly a few annoying ones there'll be dramas don't worry but everyone's polite at this stage. Fabian said we're crew on a ship we all have to work as a team I think that's a bit communist myself aren't we here to shine? He gave us each an apron a plain black apron he said we'll get our proper uniforms soon we've got to earn them first a workbook for writing things down and each three knives a chef's knife quite big a boning knife very bendy a paring knife very short for fiddly things we have to keep them sharp. That chef's knife felt good in my hand. Monday Tuesday Wednesday we chopped all day onions and garlic and learned how to sharpen our knives. Thursday we went out to the garden.

Well. If you've ever seen one of those pictures in one of those magazines you might have seen one of those stone houses with one of those kitchen gardens an old wooden fence a bloke in a beret now you've got an idea of our garden here. There's even a gate. Summer so everything's coming on the bees the butterflies vegetables herbs flowers you can use flowers for cooking I didn't know that all in rows and all the rows in sections Fabian explained it all. If that there is your workshop he said pointing back at the kitchen then this here is your storehouse. Close your eyes he said. Listen he said. Smell now taste. He was handing each of us with our eyes closed a tiny ball I could feel it in my hand smooth and warm. Put it in your mouth he said.

Well it was obvious straightaway it was a little tomato but not like those ones you see in those plastic boxes in the supermarket this was a little tomato like you've never tasted it burst in your mouth all juicy and sweet a tingle on your tongue and all the rotten tastes you ever had were gone. Now everyone open your eyes Fabian said. The sun said Fabian the soil the water those butterflies jumping around on the flowers all this made that little ball this is your resource this is nature this is your storehouse. I don't think there was anyone who didn't think that was the best tomato they ever tasted and who when they opened their eyes didn't look at Fabian with their tongues hanging out.

Next Fabian told us about growing how you don't just

stick things in the ground and hope you've got to let nature work for you for example put basil with tomatoes Fabian said because the smell will keep away the pests and marigolds too they're a flower this is called complementary planting. Now rotation I'll explain rotation rotation means not putting a vegetable in the same bed you put it in last year so the diseases of that vegetable don't stay in the soil and make the next crop sick so you rotate the different kinds of vegetables between the beds for example you have four different types of vegetables fruit leaf legumes and root so you make four beds.

Now fruit is like tomatoes and things like zucchinis and cucumbers which are fruits and leaf is like lettuces and cabbage and legumes are beans and peas and root are carrots and that sort of thing so each has a different bed. So if for example I had four beds and I put for example in the first year say fruit in the first and leaf in the second and legumes in the third and root in the fourth then the next year you see I'd put root in the first and fruit in the second and leaf in the third and legumes in the fourth because fruit was first and root was last but now root is first you see? But that's not all I say four beds but there are really five because the fifth you have to leave fallow which means you don't put anything in it. So after root in the fourth in the first year you actually have the fifth which is fallow.

But you don't want to leave the same bed fallow all the time so you have to rotate that too so if like I said in the first year fruit was in the first and leaf in the second and legumes in the third and root in the fourth and the fifth was fallow then what you should do now is move fallow to the first where your tomatoes and zucchinis say were. So fallow in the first fruit in the second leaf in the third legumes in the fourth and root in the fifth which was fallow. Then in the second year root in the first fruit in the second no that's not right fallow in the second fruit in the third no that's not right I'm lost doesn't matter. But you rotate your crops you see and the same bit of ground will feed a whole village this is what Fabian said anyway.

So that was the rotation. We spent a long time out in the garden it was very beautiful not like ours at home pebble paving and geraniums this was everything mixed up together and you know what I know this sounds silly but everything mixed up looked happy.

Near the end of our garden time Fabian said now I want you to go around and pick yourself a selection of vegetables just a few and herbs whatever you like you are going to use them tonight. Everyone was confused some I reckon even scared they didn't know what to pick they thought there was a right or wrong vegetable but Fabian smiled and said there is no right or wrong cooking is about inspiration and inspiration doesn't have rules. That was a really big thing Fabian said and see I've remembered it now. They were stupid those kids to ask about right or wrong I didn't I picked garlic carrots a green onion beans and three different herbs I didn't know their names. Fabian gave me a piece of string and told me to tie the herbs together. When we got back inside we put our things in the coolroom wrapped in clingwrap our names texta'd on them then Fabian said all right now let's go and meet Terry.

Terry is the caretaker here a rough guy in his fifties short and nuggetty a leathery face a Tigers cap very old and oily like it's from 1980 he was carrying an axe. Fabian said there was nothing Terry didn't know about the beasts of the earth and the birds of the air and every green herb he meant all the animals and plants. Terry was going to show us how to kill a chook but no you don't call it a chook you call it a bird and you don't buy those things from the supermarket they pump them up with chemicals that make girls get their periods early. We followed Terry to the chookpen on the other side of the garden beside it the big black plastic tanks for the trout the pump humming all day long. Here we are said Terry. There was a rickety old gate with a top latch chicken wire all round a roosting shed at one end Terry stood in front of the gate we all gathered around Fabian stood off to one side.

Who's ever done the chicken dance? said Terry. He was a funny bloke all right. A couple of people put up their hands and Terry said well here's a chicken dance you've probably never seen and he lifted the latch and opened the gate and started chasing the chooks I mean birds around until one just sort of ran into his hands. He held it up squawking and flapping and that's when everyone realised what he meant. Some of the kids went squeamish then it was quick when he did it.

There was a stump near the gate and beside that a wooden bench wham with the axe and off with the head. We watched for a while it ran around and around the dance was not all that special in my opinion soon we were learning how to pluck it. There was an old tin bucket next to the bench Terry laid the bird on the bench the dead neck hanging down and let the blood drip into it drip drip drip.

Now he said who'd like to have a go at plucking? It was a dumb-faced kid who put up his hand he said his name was Luke. All right Luke you'll do said Terry come here. The idea with plucking is you start from the tail and work against the grain towards the head but like Terry said you've got to be careful not to tear the skin. Luke was pretty hopeless but none of us would have been much better most didn't know a chook had feathers let alone how to pluck them. Good try said Terry back to the pine now son and I'll show you.

Well honestly you've never seen anything like it Terry plucking that bird on that bench I've never seen anything like it myself. In less than a minute there was only a bit of fluff left then he gets a little gas torch from under the bench like Dad used to use for soldering and he lights the flame and blasts the bird with it. After a while he turned off the torch and held the bird up by the feet all the fluff and feathers gone the skin still smoking. Whala! he said. Now I'll hand you over to Fab. Terry cleaned the bench brushed the feathers into the bucket then he went to the tap at the corner of the pen and started washing his hands.

The flies were already swarming around the dead bird on the bench it hardly looked like a bird anymore more like some weird alien. Fabian stepped forward he had a chef's knife in his hand a beautiful-looking thing a big wide blade a pointy end and a sharpening steel in a sheath. He smiled and said thank you Terry. Terry said no worries I love killing things and everybody laughed. Now said Fabian the nitty-gritties we've got our carcass so what do we do now? Some of the kids were getting bored it was hot out there in the sun we had been at it all morning it was two o'clock we hadn't had lunch. Terry stood close to Fabian brushing away the flies Fabian talked very fast he worked fast too nearly as fast as Terry had plucked.

First if we are going to use this bird no matter what for he said we need to draw it this means taking the gizzards out he turned the bird on its back and with his knife he cut a nice clean cut along the neck and took out the windpipe I suppose that's what it was a long wormy thing then he made a cut down near its bum and pulled the gizzards out too. In Roman times said Fabian the priests would tell the future with chickens' entrails maybe even go to war because of what they said. He handed the chook guts to Terry a big handful and Terry took them over to the bucket but before he dropped them in he held them up and looked at them all funny like he was playing a Roman priest. I see many famous chefs! he said and everybody laughed again. Now said Fabian we will joint it.

I won't tell you about all the jointing it's very complicated but anyway by the end you would have recognised it we had drumsticks wings breasts and a carcass for making soup. Fabian laid them all out on the bench it did look impressive all that coming from one chook that ten minutes before was scratching around in its pen. I felt sorry for its relatives watching all this they could only watch with one eye it was too much to watch with two. All right said Fabian so that's our chicken one of our staple ingredients after lunch this is what we are going to cook. Terry killed five more birds we watched from a distance at the outside tables eating cold meat and salad it was slaughter.

When we went back to the kitchen after lunch Fabian had the chickens jointed on a bench in piles. Now go and get your garden things he said and bring them back here he meant our vegetables and herbs. All right he said now choose your workstation and take a chicken portion each enough for a meal for two. Well! Everyone was so confused going this way and that thinking OK now Fabian is going to give us a recipe and show us how to cook but no the idea was to get inspired. I took a spot at the bench next to Hunter Josh the fat kid next to him Lachlan the skinny kid with spiky hair next to me. Now said Fabian look at your ingredients. I had one drumstick one wing one breast garlic carrots that green onion was called a leek beans and herbs. Look carefully said Fabian let your imagination work. I kept looking for a while. Next Fabian said to choose our pots or pans or whatever we thought we needed from the shelves. Chaos again but not so bad because this time lots of people probably half just stood at their benches looking stupid. I chose a heavy pot I could hardly lift it a ladle and a big wooden spoon. Hunter had a frying pan and saucepan.

Well the short and sweet of it was that for the next hour and a half thirteen people from the wrong side of the tracks tried to make food they thought people from the right side of the tracks would like to eat and nearly busted their guts trying. Drunks potheads thieves. Dickheads. Fabian was there to help but one to thirteen's not a good ratio as soon as he finished with one person someone else was yelling him over. I got off to an OK start I chopped the garlic leek and carrot like I'd learnt and cooked them in a bit of oil I had the heat down low I had no idea what I was doing. That's good said Fabian coming over let them sweat before you add your meat don't put your *bouquet garni* in until last. It was only because when he said that he looked down at my bunch of herbs that I knew he meant my bunch of herbs was a *bouquet garni*. And this he said and he put half a bottle of white wine on the bench. Half a cup he said then reduce it he didn't say anything else.

Well I won't go on about it I'm not big-noting but let's just say that out of thirteen students and thirteen dishes there was only one you could eat. Fabian got everyone to gather around my bench and look at my pot then he asked me what I used and what I did. There have not been many big moments in my life the goal I kicked in Under 14s the wooden pencil box in Year 10 getting off on good behaviour but for me this was a triumph. Fabian plated it up you call it plating up a big white plate bigger than I've ever seen one chicken breast then a wing at an angle a ladle of vegetables and last a swirl of the ladle so you got a splash and some drips of browny-greeny-yellow autumn-looking sauce. Here he said and he gave me a fork chef's first taste it was a proud smile he gave me. I tore off a little bit of the breast with the fork and stabbed a bit of carrot I was careful to hold it like a fork not a shovel and I put the food in my mouth.

What do you think? said Fabian. It needs a bit of salt I said. Fabian smiled at that. Everyone get a fork he said.

Fresh ingredients good preparation inspiration imagination it doesn't take much that simple formula is what has made our friend here's chicken such an outstanding success. But as you heard it wasn't perfect no dish is ever perfect I have been cooking for seventeen years and I have still not served the perfect dish. There are a lot of things I hope you will remember from today Terry our slaughtering plucking drawing and jointing the relationship between ingredients one feeding into the other and the other into the one the use of herbs here a *bouquet garni* yes write it down but above all what I want you to remember is *a bit of salt*.

No-one knew what Fabian meant but I knew he meant I knew my chicken dish was not perfect and that even while I was serving it up I was thinking of ways to improve it. This is the search for perfection me and Hunter talked about it after this is what cooking's about. That night in my bunk I couldn't sleep thinking about the day but most of all what Fabian said *a bit of salt.* Little steps he said that's another thing I will be a great chef one day.

So that was Thursday Friday we did theory mostly I was very tired the history of the chook I mean chicken I mean bird the Greeks served them at their feasts the afternoon we spent in the garden weeding and mulching. I like it outdoors it's a good life here. Fabian said you can do that recipe with vinegar instead of white wine.

Anyway Saturday all quiet not doing much but underneath all anxious because Fabian had told us Head Chef was coming tomorrow and we would have our first class with him Monday. I didn't sleep that night worrying most chefs don't sleep much some hardly at all then Sunday morning about eleven I was sitting in the sun outside the bunkhouse doing nothing a few others out there too when we heard the car pull up a man's voice then a woman's then two kids saying can we play? You can't see the house from the compound there's a high fence all round it went quiet after that they must have gone inside but then about one o'clock we heard Fabian and we guessed Head Chef talking low out in the backyard. They'd lit the barbecue there was the sound of sizzling and the smell of cooked meat and rosemary I could tell it was rosemary I had that in my *bouquet garni*. After a while we heard the wife and kids out there too the kids splashing in the pool.

After lunch which was chicken and lettuce sandwiches me and Hunter went up the hill the kids' voices drifting to us on the breeze. You could see everything from up there all the way to the road the cut-off tractor tyres painted white the long driveway the row of pines the path to the front door the old tree the bunkhouse the big kitchen over to the left. We saw Fabian coming out of the kitchen with a bottle of wine walking across the gravel area towards the back gate of the house and in the backyard walking away from us Head Chef's wife in a yellow bikini. Me and Hunter both went quiet then until Hunter made one of his jokes.

Me and Hunter sat for a long time up on the hill while all of that went on down below. Some people might have been humiliated I think Hunter was in a way two guys eating their orchard apples watching the rich sip their wine but not me. While Hunter babbled on I sank deep inside myself the kids screaming and laughing adult voices smooth jazz playing the house lit by a strong sun under a big blue sky. Head Chef started out just like me I thought but he worked his way up took no shit I'm a nobody sure but if he can get it why can't I? Somewhere sometime he sat up on a hill or in a tree and looked down and asked why can't I have that and how do I get it? That night in the bunkhouse I couldn't get the pictures to fade.

Monday up early a beautiful day first thing I went to the

chookpen to get some eggs. Fabian told me if you get them early and give them to Gary he'll use them for breakfast otherwise he'll use the out-of-date ones from the coolroom the worst scrambled eggs you could imagine. Terry was up early too filling the water trough a real rough-nut like Dad I guess in the early days before he got sick and pale. I saw you watching that day with the chook said Terry. It took me a while to realise he was talking to me. Yeah I never seen that before I said. Where are you from? said Terry. I told him. That's nice out there he said. It's crap out there I said no jobs no fun no nothing. Terry laughed at that. So how come you ended up here? he said. I said it was a long story he didn't ask again.

That bird there he said with the funny foot she's the egg-queen she lays in that corner if you want to make something special get one of hers. He turned off the tap opened the latch and let himself out while I gathered the eggs a dozen in all the one he said on top. There was steam coming out of the louvre windows at the bathroom end of the bunkhouse the sun was warm now on my back a few kids sitting outside at the tables I took the eggs to the kitchen. Gary was putting his apron on a grumpy prick all right it was hard to think of him as a cook let alone a chef he should have been picking peas in Korumburra a ferret face a rat tail mullet a goatee beard a side tooth missing. Who told you to get them he said. I said no-one told me even though Fabian did. I had butterflies in my stomach Gary must have known. Big day today he said.

Soon we were eating some of us in the dining room some at the tables outside scrambled eggs with bacon and tomato on the side. You could feel the nerves all right everyone thinking I hope he doesn't pick on me. About seven-thirty Fabian came by all smiles I could hear him messing around in the kitchen then eight on the dot the last of us putting our dishes in the washer Fabian says all right people everyone to their stations please! We put on our black aprons tucked in our side towels laid out our knives we must have looked funny all neat and standing to attention but really just dropkicks we didn't have a clue.

I'm not sure what I thought Head Chef would look like but one thing for sure like they say about people on the telly he looked shorter in real life. He had his chef's gear on the white jacket side-buttoned all the way up dark trousers black clogs short-cut grey hair black-framed glasses you know the ones architects have them. He was in his forties early forties probably and now standing next to Fabian in front of the whiteboard and Fabian's not tall he only came up to his shoulder. Fabian introduced him I didn't really hear what he was saying I was looking at Head Chef trying to see who this guy really was what he was like when he was eighteen behind the cologne and the skincare products and yes I thought really he's just like me so why can't I be like him?

I missed the start Fabian was telling us Head Chef's background how he had no formal training began at the bottom spent time overseas with some of the big chefs there.

Head Chef was listening to all this with his hands clasped in front of him. He had a look that says it's no big deal but I knew that of course he was proud and already I liked that in him he had pride when did any of us in that shitkicking suburb ever have any pride? Fabian told us how Head Chef had set it up from scratch this kitchen he pointed around built and equipped from scratch exactly to Head Chef's specifications. Fabian stepped aside and Head Chef stood in his spot. I wonder what Fabian thinks of him are they close? After that we didn't know what to do someone started clapping we all clapped until Head Chef told us to stop.

I can't remember everything he said but here's what I can. He started by quoting a Frenchman I've just looked him up *Tell me what you eat and I'll tell you who you are* which means I think if you eat McDonald's you're a McDonald's person if you eat tofu and beanshoots you're that. And if said Head Chef we are what we eat would we rather serve mediocre food to mediocre people or raise society up? No-one had an answer to that. Personally said Head Chef I want to make this a better world for my children this is what the gastronomic revolution is about we *can* become better smarter healthier more successful people and surely our job our *duty* as chefs he said getting quite heated and red in the face no matter where we come from the wilds of the suburbs a house and land package a caravan park is not to say *I'm only this* but to ask *How can I be better?*

I started from nothing said Head Chef no name no fortune no press nothing at all pushing burgers around a grill at Hungry Jack's carrying tubs of oil from the storeroom the manager whacking me across the back of the head. I didn't get from there to here by settling for second best. I own three restaurants it's no big deal Melbourne Sydney one just opened in Dubai another soon in Singapore. Did I do that by trading in the mediocre? No. Mediocrity suburbananity the boring the bland this is what is holding this country back if we want to become a richer more sophisticated people we have to aim high then higher again if we don't if *you* don't I'm talking to you we'll end up all of us crawling back through the decades to the fifties cooking boring food in our boring kitchens in our boring suburban homes. If your mum's making lemon risotto with her own stock serving it with a rocket salad I'm sorry don't fool yourself into thinking she's sophisticated we've moved on risotto is a decade old at least I wouldn't walk through the door of a restaurant with risotto on the menu your mum's a sheep. But we're not sheep are we I won't have sheep in my school my school is for those who want to rise above the copycat recipe in the magazine on the table in the waiting room at the dentist's. Tomorrow and tomorrow and tomorrow. The cutting edge this edge he held up a knife that's where I want us to be out there where it's dangerous where it's risky where it hurts.

His face was very red now there were sweat beads all over his forehead everyone was very quiet Fabian had his chin up we didn't know what to do were we supposed to clap? Even before we had the chance Head Chef turned around and pulled open the coolroom door. He needs to cool off said Hunna right up close to my ear I wanted to laugh but no way I would. Head Chef was in there for a while Fabian kept standing with his chin in the air a long awkward silence it seemed to go on forever. After a while Head Chef came out kicking the sliding door closed with his foot. He was carrying a green milk crate I couldn't see what was in it.

Head Chef went to one of the middle benches everyone parted like the Red Sea no-one wanted to get too close this was the guy in the Sunday papers he put the milk crate down and started emptying it out onto the bench. But you wouldn't believe it they were packets of chops the ones you get in the supermarket a black plastic tray clingwrap on the top a thing for the blood in the bottom ten packets four chops in each. Head Chef put them on the bench in two piles of five. All right he said begin!

Everyone was totally confused now I certainly was then someone the tall kid Jordan picked up a packet tore off the clingwrap took the two chops out and took them back to his station. Head Chef was still standing there arms folded Fabian's eyes darting watching what everyone was doing. Jordan went to the coolroom and opened the door. A few others got the hint and started picking up their chops then Jordan came back out with a bunch of vegetables potatoes broccoli carrots and put them on his bench and that's when Hunter and me thought we better join in too. There was no point waiting Head Chef and Fabian weren't saying anything. We split a packet of chops between us took them back to our stations then went to the coolroom for our vegies.

There were lots of fresh vegetables in there all in milk crates in a row Terry must have picked them early. I found the ones I wanted garlic carrots leeks and beans it worked last time with the chicken I thought no reason not with the chops. Hunter was going to do his seared with buttered potatoes and beans. We all got set up at our stations I spent a while on my prep like painting said Fabian it's all in the prep then after a while I went outside to get my herbs.

Back in the kitchen no talk just the sound of chopping frying metal pans clanking taps turning on and off the coolroom door sliding open and closed. No-one knew exactly what they were doing I mean what game Head Chef was playing but already since that first lesson with the chook the chicken the bird people were starting to get it. We knew where things were now the storeroom for example people coming out with a cup of rice say or *polenta* that's an Italian thing. Not everyone's station was as tidy as mine. We'd had a lesson on *mise en place* that's French for how you lay out all your little containers your banks of chopped herbs say or spices your garnishes your salt and pepper so you know where they are and can get them easy. It was funny watching all the different styles some very slow thinking it all through one guy already had his dish in the bin and was starting again.

Me I was pretty calm I browned the chops drained the fat sautéed the vegetables put in a cup this time of red wine and added my *bouquet garni*. I needed to cook it for at least half an hour probably longer some of the others who'd done a quick fry or grill were already plating up. Head Chef was still saying nothing wandering around the kitchen with his hands behind his back what is that with the hands behind the back it makes you stronger does it? If he came up to a station where a dish was getting plated he wouldn't say anything just sort of look down his nose like the French guys in the movies then move on. Anyway after thirty-five minutes the last ten medium-high with the lid off to reduce it I plated up wiped off and finished with a parsley garnish. Head Chef walked past and looked at my dish like one of those parking inspectors pretending you're not there. He gave Hunter's dish an even quicker glance no wonder it looked revolting then after a quick chat with Fabian at the door like a phantom he was gone.

It went quiet in the kitchen after that. It was past lunch we hadn't seen Gary he must have had the day off. We could hear Fabian fussing around in the coolroom moving pallets Head Chef had said nothing Fabian had said nothing none of us were saying anything were we supposed to throw it in the bin and start again? Anyway after a while one of us the little guy with the curly hair Rory picked up his plate and walked into the dining room on his own. The rest of us waited to see if he was going to get in trouble for that but then Fabian came out of the coolroom taking off his apron. He hung it on a hook near the door and went outside. We picked up our plates too they were getting cold and followed Rory into the dining room.

Well I tell you what that was really strange in there us all eating like that with our aprons still on it felt like the dining room in prison maybe after they've put down a riot the clink of cutlery the sound of chewing thirteen heads trying to figure out what they're supposed to think. I ate my lamb chop casserole and let me tell you it stank. What worked for the chook didn't work for the chop I could hardly eat it there was a scum on top no flavour it was just fatty mush. I spent a long time watching the scum go hard.

Next morning Fabian came into the kitchen bang on eight all fresh and ready to go it was like Head Chef had never been there. He drew a picture of a cow on the board a pig then a sheep then he circled the sheep and rubbed out the cow and the pig then he drew an arrow from the sheep's behind and drew a mini-sheep which after a while we realised was a lamb. Then he rubbed out the sheep. We are going to talk about lamb he said one of our most delicious and at the same time versatile meats.

Well. I was slow to catch up at first but I think this is when I first started to really understand the history of food gastronomy they call it as opposed to just eating. We buy those lamb chops from the supermarket or the butcher and we think I don't know I know this sounds silly we are the first ones ever to eat a lamb chop or a rack but no in the Bible they sacrificed them so they weren't just mini-sheep they were something special in Greece in Italy too and in Egypt. Fabian painted a word picture for us he was good at that of a feast in Greece where they started with the head can you imagine boiled up with herbs and spices and wine and the guests would pick bits of meat off it with their fingers then after that the rest of it roasted over the coals the whole thing on the table where the servants would joint and carve it. This was a sacred animal said Fabian the day before its throat would have been cut by the priestess at the temple as an offering to the gods what these people were eating was connecting them to something outside themselves something greater this is what food was to them.

It was good the way Fabian talked everyone standing at their stations all eyes all ears the longer we listened the further yesterday's drama faded we felt safe with Fabian we were being led somewhere not getting thrown to the lions like with Head Chef. After that Fabian drew a diagram on the whiteboard a lamb cut into bits with numbers on it number one the shoulder number two and three the neck number four five six the back and so on. Copy this into your workbooks he said I had mine some of the others didn't they went back to the bunkhouse to get them.

After that I mean after we'd all copied the drawing into our workbooks we had to close them and Fabian made us repeat. He had a wooden spoon he pointed with the handle I really felt like I was back at school now primary school one bit of the lamb at a time we had to say what it was called this is Fabian mind you who only a few days before was talking about inspiration and imagination and here we were like a bunch of preps learning our ABCs. We did it for nearly four hours I was still repeating it *neck shoulder loin chump leg breast* when I went to bed that night. The next day we had a test no-one did very well then we went over it all again after lunch. *What would you do with the best end of neck? Where does the backstrap come from? What bones are you removing when you butterfly a leg?*

At the end of class on Wednesday me and Hunter took our workbooks up the hill away from everyone and started testing each other out. It was weird up there still hot very muggy the sun low the light all yellow the voices in the yard. Head Chef and his wife had guests they must have arrived that afternoon we could see a new car in the drive behind Head Chef's Audi and hear them all talking and laughing. Me and Hunter kept our heads down one asking questions the other answering. Who would have thought I thought me who this time last month could barely make a bowl of nachos learning by rote in French the three principal methods of preparation or the difference between a shank and a shoulder? Yes I thought of all the doors I could have opened I have opened the right one good food good wine fine dining learn how to arrange beautiful food on a plate and a beautiful world is yours. That's what I thought anyway sitting up there on the hill the guests below all drinking and laughing Head Chef down there too his secret safe bigger than the side-buttoned jacket the glasses the waxy skin the cologne. Beautiful food beautifully presented yes that's the key to the door.

Me and Hunter didn't spare the horses studying lamb up there on the hill it was nearly dark when we came back down. The noise from the house was louder now they were really enjoying themselves on the way to the dining room we met Fabian coming out of the kitchen carrying two bottles of wine. How's it going boys he said very friendly the hard taskmaster and now all smiley and nice. Dinner was quiet afterwards a few boys playing cards others on the computer writing emails home. In the kitchen Gary was packing up the last of his things he had a wife to go home go to tracky-dacks crop-top a swallow tattoo forequarter chops peas and mash warming on a pot on the stove she was probably already on her second chardonnay. We heard the old Mitsubishi start up.

After me and Hunter finished the dishes it was our turn to do them I went to the coolroom and turned on the light a hundred watt bulb in the ceiling. The green milk crate was still in there pushed up against the wall the leftover packets of meat still in it I took one out and poked the chops through the clingwrap. Maybe they were a bit fatty but Fabian had told us a bit of fat is good trimmed lamb dries out he said. I went back to the bunkhouse went to bed early but I couldn't get the mystery of the chops out of my head. Why did Head Chef walk out like that? What did we do wrong?

Thursday we were finishing our breakfast when Fabian came over. He had a hangover for sure. No class this morning he said I've arranged for you to see Terry does everyone know where the main shed is? It was on the other side of the hill. All right said Fabian off you go I'll meet you back here later. We all set off. We could hear Head Chef's kids already up splashing in the pool. The ruts were deep in places a barbed-wire fence a paddock on one side black cows grazing out there all still and silent. We were a motley bunch all right world-class chefs we looked like we belonged in a bus shelter.

The track wound its way round the edge of the hill and pretty soon we could see a big tin shed three walls a roof the front part open bits of machinery scattered around a diesel tank on a stand to one side. Come on kiddies Terry shouted. We could see someone else near the ute in the yard a girl in tight jeans *land ho!* said Hunter poking me in the ribs. Twenty-two maybe or twenty-three good-looking too which was hard to believe Terry's got a face like a primate. This is my daughter Rose he said. She had big hips big bosoms long dark hair and a slow way of moving her smile a half-smile like she was keeping some to herself. She went inside the shed behind a partition wall and turned the radio on. All right gentlemen said Terry thirteen guys looking at his daughter's butt excuse me for interrupting but I understand you've been learning about lamb now it may come as a surprise to you I'll get the smelling salts ready but that white thing in the back of the ute there that is one. We all turned we hadn't noticed tied to the roll bar with a rope a lamb the cutest thing you've ever seen. And then like the cartoons when the light bulb goes on I saw what this was about. Even with the picture on the whiteboard with all the bits numbered one to ten none of us not one of us had been able to get it into our heads that a lamb is a woolly four-legged thing like the thing on the rope in the back of Terry's ute. Lamb chops don't come from a packet they come from a lamb this was our first lesson today.

Terry untied the rope and lifted the lamb like a kid with a new puppy two arms under the belly out of the ute. He handed the rope to a guy called Daniel pale and twitchy that guy's had drug trouble for sure. Take it for a walk said Terry go on walk it up and down. He made us all do this take the rope walk the lamb we all knew what was coming we weren't stupid. Terry took out a knife from the front of the ute the blade all worn how many lambs must he have killed with that? Bring it here he said to Luke the dumb-faced kid the last person with the rope bring it over here he was pointing to a spot on one side of the shed we could see the ground stained with old blood. He had a dish like the ones you drain sump oil into he set it on the ground. Over here he said and he took the rope the lamb knew what was coming fear in all the genes it started pulling twisting its head digging in its heels.

Come on little fella said Terry which only made it worse some of the kids were thinking about their baby brothers or sisters I was thinking about how much blood and how red it was going to be. Come on little fella said Terry he had a handful of skin now he slipped the rope over the lamb's head kicked its legs out from under it and laid it down on its side. Next he kicked the dish underneath put his knee on the lamb it was bleating now save me save me I done nothing wrong pulled its head back and ran the knife across its throat very tight and clean. The blood came out straightaway a big spurt that missed the dish. Terry cut a few more times back and forth I heard someone behind me faint someone caught him. Terry hacked a couple more times the blood glooping into the dish the lamb spasmed its little legs jiggling its eyes wide open you could see it thinking I wonder what then it went very still. Terry wiped the blade on the wool.

There was about a third of a dish of blood now Rose was helping the kid who fainted lucky him. Terry picked the lamb up by its hind legs the head dangling down on half a neck and dragged it into the shed where he hung it head-down on a triangle tepee sort of frame. Can you bring that here he said meaning the dish one of the kids brought it in juggling it so it wouldn't spill and put it under the lamb's head. All right said Terry so we've slaughtered our lamb this is what is called a spring lamb ten weeks old milk-fed no pasture the flesh pale pink no grassiness to it which is what you get with grazing lamb.

All right he said so next we're going to skin the little fella are you all right there now he said to the kid who fainted he was on a chair his head between his knees. Terry smiled and gave us a wink as if we were any better we weren't. He went over to the wall and turned an air compressor on. He blasted the gauge a few times to make sure it was working then went back to the lamb hanging on the frame and made a little cut near its bum. He put the nozzle in squeezed the trigger and the lamb started blowing up like a balloon. Everyone was going ugh and agh the kid on the chair looked up then straight-away he put his head down again. This will get the skin away from the carcass Terry said and make it easier to get off. He hung the gauge back on the hook the lamb three times its normal size we could hear a slow leak from the cut. Terry was working fast now no words we just watched it was awesome. He cut around the bum put a flat hand in between the meat and the skin and started pushing the skin away working all the way down cutting around each of the legs to release them crouching down and pulling the skin off over its head. He held the skin up for us to see then threw it on the back of a chair.

What was left on the frame was a weird alien creature pink and purple and grey and white Terry had turned it from a lamb into something else we didn't know what but already we could see how that cute little fluffy animal in the back of the ute was becoming a thing we could eat. All right said Terry show's over folks we'll let him hang here for a couple of hours best scenario would be a couple of days but Fab wants to get to work on it with you jokers this afternoon. Are you all right there now? The sick guy nodded and stood up. A round of applause said Terry for the resurrection of Jesus he clapped but only a few others clapped too. Rose gave her dad a tut-tut look she was nice I liked her not just because she was a girl.

After lunch when we went back into class no-one ate or just ate a bit no-one was hungry understandable really the dead lamb was on the bench and Fabian was sharpening his knife. He had a steely look about him. All right he said we are going to butcher this animal and later you will need to iden-tify the cuts for me and show me how you might use them. Still no sign of Head Chef. Fabian shuffled his sharpening steel one more time over his knife which was short and very pointy. First thing he did was attack the neck I mean he actu-ally stabbed and hacked until the head came off on the floor beside the bench was a plastic tub he dropped the head into it with a thump.

Next he moved to the other end and started taking off the leg sometimes stabbing sometimes slicing till in the end he had a leg of lamb he put that aside for us to see. He did the same with the other leg next he got a hacksaw and cut off the ribs both sides the thin end with the meat still on you can bone them roll them stuff them roast them they are very nice apparently. He put the breast aside and went back to the neck cut the scrag end off that's the small bit close to the head he put that in the tub then he sawed again the saddle that's the big bit the main bit the middle neck the best end the shoulder he put them in a row on the bench then sawed the saddle in two that was two loins and trimmed the ribs. All the cuts so far he pushed to the end of the bench so there was just one loin left. A few quick cuts and Fabian had eight lamb chops he pushed four of these aside into a pile arranged the other four in a row leaned down under the bench got the green milk crate and took out a supermarket packet. He tore off the clingwrap took out the four chops and arranged them on the bench next to the others.

It was funny some of the kids were still writing in their workbooks or looking at the board not everyone had cottoned on yet you could see the difference the four from the packet dry and grey the four from the carcass fleshy and pink. Everyone was gathering around the bench now poking the chops no-one had even noticed Fabian was gone until someone turned to ask him a question and that's when we realised Head Chef was standing in the door. He was dressed in his civvies a snappy brown suit with a black t-shirt underneath his skin very shiny his wife and kids beside him. She was beautiful like a model a lot taller than him not much make-up getting on though I reckon she'd had a bit of work done around the eyes she had a kid holding each hand.

Well what could we say it was like at school when you're shooting spit balls. All of us we couldn't help it we parted either side of the bench standing to attention so Head Chef had a view of the eight chops in two groups of four lying on it. He had a sort of smile I think it was a smile it was hard to tell. Well gentlemen he said he called us gentlemen I hope you have had a useful couple of days Fabian tells me you've been studying lamb. Everyone nodded like idiots a couple even pointed at the whiteboard like they were saying yes Chef and there's our lamb picture there. Head Chef took a couple of steps forward and we all leaned a couple of centimetres back. And tell me said Head Chef pointing you what did you learn about lamb this week? It was no accident it was like the lion chasing the weakest gazelle till it slips and falls Head Chef was pointing at Daniel the drug kid he looked like he didn't know his own name let alone what he'd learnt about lamb. What is the first principle of a successful lamb dish Head Chef was asking taking another couple of steps forward Daniel looked like he was going to die. Take your time said Head Chef we have all the time in the world. Daniel certainly took his time but eventually because he had to say something even though he had no idea what to say and because he'd vaguely remembered something from Tuesday's class he said pepper. You could have heard a pin drop Head Chef looked at Daniel's feet then he turned and gave his wife a signal very subtle just a nod of the head. She turned the kids around and closed the door behind her.

Head Chef didn't do anything yet he was waiting till they were gone you could hear their feet on the gravel outside then as if some sound in particular had given him his cue he turned to the bench and picked up a supermarket chop in one hand a fresh one in the other and what's the word deliberately brought one then the other up to his nose like an elevator up then down. Now he gestured for Daniel to step forward Daniel was shitting himself we could all see how he moved his feet like his shoes had lead in them until he was a step closer to the chops. Head Chef lifted each chop to Daniel's nose and Daniel sniffed them almost with a thought bubble question in front of his forehead going yes Chef but what am I smelling them *for*?

Head Chef took them away Daniel's thought bubble still hanging there and now and this really freaked him out one at a time Head Chef put a chop to his own cheek first the supermarket then the freshly slaughtered one he was feeling flesh on flesh not how fresh they looked but *felt*. Daniel knew what to do this time he turned sideways and offered his cheek to the chops. Head Chef didn't ask any more questions he stood there with the two chops flat on the palm of each hand like the innocent and guilty on the scales of justice then so fast that at first we didn't know what had happened he hurled the supermarket chops at the far wall one two three four the third went straight through the servery window into the dining room where we heard it hit the wall with a slap. Next everything happened so fast it's hard to remember it all in the right order without leaving anything out.

Head Chef took a skillet from the hook above the stove turned the jet up high put the skillet on and poured olive oil into it. He was still in his suit. From the coolroom very fast he brought butter and from a shelf at one of the other stations half a bottle of red wine. He asked Hunna because Hunna was standing near to get two sprigs of rosemary from the garden now you have no idea how fast he took a knife picked the best chop and trimmed the bone so it was now just a bone to hold and a juicy little bit of meat at the end very small a thin layer of creamy fat on the edge. He turned the oven on put a plate in it Hunna came back running Head Chef stripped a rosemary sprig and chopped it very fast and fine. He seasoned the chop with salt and pepper put it on the skillet it went berserk oil and flame going everywhere and cooked it one minute each side. Then he took the warm plate out of the oven put the chop in the middle put the skillet back on the flame threw in the chopped rosemary a splash of wine a bit of butter turned the jet down stirred that through brought the skillet to the plate poured the juice it's called *jus* onto the chop put the other sprig of rosemary on gave it some black pepper and slid it onto the bench in the centre of the room.

He'd wrecked his suit there was oil spattered all over it he was wiping his hands on a tea-towel big beads of sweat on his forehead his glasses had gone all cloudy. All right he said gentlemen pan-seared lamb cutlet with a rosemary and red wine *jus* spring lamb freshly slaughtered briefly hung two minutes prep three minutes cooking now that gentlemen is a dish I would be happy to serve my customers those other pieces of crap I wouldn't feed to my dog. So again he said what is the first principle of a successful lamb dish? But even if Daniel had figured it out Head Chef didn't give him the chance to answer. Fresh ingredients honesty in the preparation food cooked not with the head but with the heart. He was walking around the bench we were getting dizzy watching him I couldn't believe he did that to his suit I mean it would have cost thousands there was no way you could clean it and all the time he was walking he was talking.

Why are you here he was saying that is the question I ask myself did you put yourself up for this because your parents or your case workers told you to or because you actually want to make something of yourselves? No-one was sure if this was a question Head Chef needed an answer to we all sort of shuffled and looked the other way.

Let me give you a little history lesson he said it took us a while to realise that's what he meant that he was going to give us a history lesson and we were going to listen. Twenty or so years ago he said when you weren't even born the world was divided into two the communists on one side bad the capitalists on the other side good and down the middle a thing called the Iron Curtain to keep the two sides apart. Now gentlemen there were many things the communists on the other side of the Curtain didn't have but the one thing they wanted most was *freedom*. Freedom to make something of themselves. Now. You jokers here have the great honour to be brought up in a world where there are no walls no barriers no good or bad there is only freedom a world where choice is not a privilege but a right. Those behind the Curtain said Head Chef couldn't accumulate wealth buy stocks and shares invest in property everything had to be *shared*. You on the other hand yes I'm talking to you you are a privileged generation you can get what you want if you're prepared to go out and climb that ladder of opportunity.

Head Chef's mobile rang. He took it out looked at it pushed a button and the ringing stopped. But he said looking up again I understand that in this world of freedom there are always going to be some people left behind a good system's never perfect. I know where you come from I come from there too there are no jobs in the factory suburbs the factories have all closed. But why I ask myself given this opportunity here at Cook School do some of you seem to think you're still standing at a conveyor belt? That's not what we are doing here gentlemen we have cheap Asian labour to do that. This is a *service* industry. We *serve*. Our customers don't want chops they can buy from a supermarket that's the whole point don't you see we are giving these people a dining experience they come to us looking for new ways to spend their money it is up to us to help them out.

Power through service this is your motto. By subjugating ourselves we become strong. And to what do we subjugate ourselves? To public taste. To whim. To folly. To whatever looks and smells new. We bow to the fickle and frivolous we are servants of all that is decadent excessive unnecessary. What is your role? Simple. To get your customer to pay ten times what your produce is worth and thank you for the privilege. Added value. In what is the value added? In the customer's belief that the servant in the kitchen has given his all to this dish has loved it like no other and has let it go from his kitchen to the table with a heavy heart.

Head Chef stopped stalking the bench. It was a bit religious he had his arms out palms up his wedding ring was huge. You have been chosen he said each and every one of you it could have been anyone but of all the young people wandering the suburbs wasting their lives you and you only have been chosen. Do not waste this opportunity. You have a kitchen the envy of a Michelin-star restaurant the best teaching talent in the country fresh produce at your door it is up to you to use these resources and not waste them. Remember you are flying the flag for good taste gentlemen. If you're not prepared to aim high then higher again I suggest you take your supermarket chops and go and eat them with the dogs. Head Chef pointed with a flat hand at the dish on the bench it was only now I think he realised what he'd done to his suit he was looking at his sleeve you could see a vague thought pass across his face. Taste it he said meaning the chop cooling on the big white plate. Think about what you are tasting. Remember all cooking is borrowing stealing adapting others' recipes and calling them your own. Look. Taste. When I come back I will be tasting yours and I don't want to be disappointed.

I've done my best to remember what he said and how he said it he talked for a long time so I reckon I've done pretty well. As soon as he said that last bit he was gone we heard him talking to Fabian outside then the Audi start up and the sound of it driving away. Everyone was a bit shell-shocked it took a while to move we all started getting knives and forks and gathering around the bench each cutting a tiny piece of meat and trying it. It was good. Some of the kids I could see thought it was a wank such a tiny bit of meat on such a big plate after a while Fabian came in and said that was it for classes today. He went to the bench with the butchered lamb on it and started packing up all the bits. There was something sad about that I felt sorry for him how he did all the work but Head Chef got the credit. The horse does the work but the coachman is tipped I remember Dad saying that.

That evening dinner was lamb stew and mashed potato it looked like dog's vomit I couldn't eat it. Most people went to bed early it had been a big day. About eight I heard Gary's car start up and drive away I waited a while then went to the kitchen it was dark in there and quiet.

I turned the light on in the coolroom and found the lamb cuts Fabian had put away in plastic tubs stacked one on top of the other the loin chops on the bottom. I sorted through them just like Head Chef had done picked out what I thought were the best ones and took them into the kitchen.

Not everyone took Head Chef's words seriously I know but I couldn't stop thinking about what he said especially how this was our only chance to save ourselves. People are always telling me not to get ahead of myself but now I thought why not? Isn't it only the dreamers who have ever done anything in this world? We are grubs we are nothing but from there we raise ourselves up that's what Head Chef was saying anyway. If we're going to have to polish the boots of the master why not learn to polish them really well?

On the benches along the window side there was just enough moonlight to see and on one bench in particular a good strong silver light the moon outside was nearly full. I wanted to see how he did that I mean trim the chops a few swishes of the knife and it wasn't like those chops we've always eaten it was a beautiful thing the white bone the little medallion of meat. I tried the first one it was pretty bad my knife wasn't sharp enough I worked it with the steel took another one tried again each time a little better. It was weird working in the moonlight. It was my fourth chop where I really got it a nice even layer of creamy fat on one side the flesh pink and glistening like when you cut yourself fresh and vivid till the blood finally comes.

That's when I heard Fabian's voice in the doorway. Don't you think you might do better with the light on he said and he flicked on one bank of fluoros. He was in his civvies jeans and jumper the light was very bright I had to give myself a minute to see. He walked over to the storeroom and came back out with a bottle of red and two glasses. I thought he was taking them back to the house maybe he had a guest I'd never really thought about that whether he was married or had a girlfriend or what he did on his own in the house at night when Head Chef had gone back to the city. He brought the bottle over to the bench and poured two glasses he was already a bit pissed it must be hard for him sometimes. He pushed my glass towards me. The fat you took off the bone he said don't throw it away keep that bit. Go and get your other ingredients he said.

When I came back from the garden with a sprig of rosemary Fabian already had the skillet on. I gathered up the other things utensils butter salt pepper I felt nervous now. Relax said Fabian and he pointed to the other glass of wine. What did you get out of today? he said. It was weird I had no idea how I ended up like this sneaking into the kitchen to play for a while and now here I was sitting with my Sous Chef drinking.

I don't know I said it was true I didn't I guess how the right cut of meat is your starting point there's no use heating the pan if you don't have the right cut of meat.

Fabian smiled. And Head Chef he said what did you make of him? This was awkward no doubt about it. Well I said he was pretty impressive he made his point about freshness speed simplicity presentation it was all there on the plate wasn't it? Fabian smiled again. And the other things he said the bigger picture how we are servants and how making the customer happy gives us power. I've been thinking about that too I said. Fabian sipped his wine.

The skillet was smoking. There's a TV crew coming said Fabian to shoot footage for his show so he'll want to see some improvement. I said I thought that would be good having something to work towards. TV makes you or breaks you said Fabian bringing his glass to his lips we are nothing without TV. There was a long pause after that. I asked him how long he'd been in the business. I've been a Sous Chef seven years said Fabian but I've been in the business nearly twenty. I started at the bottom just like everyone he said washing dishes doing prep working the ski fields in the season. One year there was a guest chef up there he liked what he saw gave me his card told me to come and see him when I got back to the city.

Fabian went quiet. He gulped his wine and held his hand flat over the skillet. All right he said now here's a little trick get your piece of lamb fat that's belly fat the best bit fork it and swirl it around the skillet to give it a good coating it will smoke like hell but that's what you want see if you can taste the difference at the end.

So now I was really in it up to my neck I chopped my rosemary finer said Fabian laid out my ingredients seasoned my meat smoked the skillet. I won't go through it all I told you how Head Chef did it I did it like that as best I could and plated up at the end. Fabian took one taste and scraped it into the bin. Too much butter he said. Re-do! I went through three chops back to the coolroom to get more butter out to the garden to get more rosemary my station all messy Fabian the whole time on his stool telling me to do it again. I realised he was getting pissed but if he was it didn't dull his brain he was at me the whole time pointing smelling adjusting. I plated up the fourth Fabian poked it I could see his eyes sparkle he leaned over and smelled it. Taste it he said and he handed me the fork. I cut myself a little piece it was very good the flavours in harmony the meaty smell coming through but on top of that the slight acidity of the wine and the sweet perfume of the rosemary at the back of the nose. When I put down my fork Fabian raised his glass we clinked glasses he stood up no word and walked to the door. When you've finished turn out the lights he said he was slurring his words and swaying slightly there are books in the office you can borrow them any time have a look in the Larousse. Loin of lamb *bonne femme*-style he said now there's a casserole for you. Fabian stepped outside and the door closed behind him.

I stayed there a while in the kitchen. How lucky am I I thought sitting here eating pan-seared lamb with a rosemary and red wine *jus* drinking wine out of a glass with a stem the moon bright the night calm how far have I come already I thought how much further to go?

I had crossed a line *power through service* I will learn how to serve that's what I said to myself sitting there at the bench I will become a servant I will do what I am told. How'd that little man with the glasses from the crappy suburb get that beautiful wife and those beautiful kids and that beautiful car and that beautiful house the swimming pool the restaurant empire he got it by serving by smiling by bowing by taking the plate back to the kitchen and making his underlings do it again. He knows how to serve but more important he knows *who* to serve he got to the top by bowing and crawling now there's a riddle for you but true maybe all powerful people got there like that.

A 1996 Coonawarra cabernet sauvignon don't worry I was only sipping. This was not a bag of goon in the park Macca's at midnight this was dark crimson deep earth ripe berries good oak in the finish a prime cut of fresh lamb on a big white plate. Later on I cleaned up put everything away the place even quieter now but last thing before I turned out the lights I went into the office and found that book Fabian told me about a big book you could have killed a man with it it was that big.

Outside all the stars out the moon high in the sky a

light on in the bathroom at the end of the bunkhouse and one on in the main house where Fabian I suppose was having his nightcap. I could hear a bull bellowing from way over on the other side of the hill and a bird cawing somewhere. The chooks too I could hear them doing their bwark-bwark in the dark and now with my ears used to all these sounds I could hear music too Fabian must have had it on in the house. I went to the bathroom brushed my teeth took the book to bed there were a few kids still awake torches and reading lights here and there some listening to music I wondered how many were planning their escape? Hunter was asleep I climbed up onto the top bunk got under the covers and lay there clutching the big book thinking.

It was strange how calm I felt cooking had done this all my old anger melting like butter and me saying hit me kick me I don't care I am here to serve. How many times did they tell me to pull my head in well look here I am my head's in I hope they're happy cops social workers all that I'm going to do what I am told. That was the beginning of all my mistakes I never knew how to do what I was told I just didn't have it in me. But there's no point getting angry now the only person who deserves a good beating is me. As for the sneers of the do-gooders who never did any good the friends who smiled to my face and stabbed me in the back forgive everything I said forgive everything with a vengeance you have no idea how strong that made me feel.

Sunday visiting day Mum and Dad came up Dad still pretty sick coughing into his mask and Mum too fat to wheel him when I saw them coming I thought good good now I remember that's what I'm leaving behind. Head Chef and his family have gone so it's pretty quiet here now. My sister Tash couldn't come up she was too busy with the kids. We had to make a menu and serve them at the tables in the dining room not all the parents came up there were a few kids pretty quiet that night. How much effort is that really to come up and see how your kid's getting on is that so hard really? Our main dish was lamb. I did a *carré d'agneau à la bonne femme* out of the book Hunter grilled chops and veg. He introduced me to his parents I introduced him to mine his looked like they crawled out of a cave. I saw Mum looking at Dad at one point her eyebrows up like she was saying well well well but Dad was mostly concentrating on his breathing. I brought the plates to the table balanced on one arm and explained the components of my dish. *Bon appétit* I said. After lunch I helped Mum get him in the car. Leave it alone Zac she said. The others left soon after that the kids saying goodbye the cars heading home one by one. We lost another kid that day there are only twelve of us now.

Anyway Monday straight back to class like usual Head Chef and his TV crew were coming soon said Fabian and we had to choose a dish and practise for when they came. Fabian says there's something wrong with a kitchen that doesn't have a bit of tension in it and well don't worry after that there was tension all right everyone getting ingredients secretly from the garden cooking out of hours. My key ingredient was lamb I was reading the Larousse every night and any other stuff I could find online learning the breeds the cuts the methods the knives you use to get what you want the way to run your kitchen the names of your chefs the Sous Chef below you below him the Chefs de Partie and below them the Commis Chefs taking the hits. I was learning French too because cooking is a French thing you don't just say yes you say *oui* practising in the kitchen till all hours banging pots and pans scorching myself doing it over again. I was not going to screw it up this time.

Make a friend of your supplier Fabian said so every day after class before dinner me and Hunter went round the hill to the main shed to see Terry and sometimes sure I was looking for Rose I saw her a few times and even spoke to her once. The first time we went round it was late afternoon the Tuesday or Wednesday after visiting day early autumn the evenings getting cool the sky all reds and oranges a big rusty patch on the ground in front of the shed from the blood of all the lambs. I told Terry how I'd read about beef fed with grain not grass could you do the same thing with lamb? I was starting to understand you see how your product works how you can manipulate it to your needs the French stuff their geese with corn till their livers are as big as footballs you call that *foie gras*. Terry said sure he took us out to the sheep paddock the lambs following their mothers on tip-toe clouds of insects wafting up behind. He told me to pick one out while he went back to the shed for some rope.

All the little lambs all looked the same to me but when Terry came back I pointed one out and said I'll have that one there. About six weeks old said Terry that's good and still not weaned. It was funny then watching him chase it around Hunter kept doing his hunting horn tuh-tuh-tuh! and cheering when Terry got close. It was a quick little thing all right its mother bleating from a distance like mothers do Terry got the rope on it in the end. It was already getting dark when we got back to the shed Terry found an old gate and some other bits of timber and we helped him make a pen up against the inside wall of the shed. The little lamb hadn't stopped crying it was an odd sound hard to listen to Terry went in behind the partition wall a light went on then he came back out with Rose who was carrying a bottle of milk and a teat. She was wearing jeans and boots like before but this time with a big sloppy jumper you couldn't see much underneath. She put the bottle in the wire holder Terry rigged up and soon the lamb was sucking away there happy as can be. Rosie used to feed the lambs when she was a kid he said. Rose stood around for a bit with her hands in the back pockets of her jeans watching the lamb drink but then it was awkward I could see that and she went back inside.

Terry got some wood and made a fire on the concrete floor at the front of the shed. Don't go back and eat that weasel's slops he said stay for dinner here when the coals are red we'll have trout with baked potatoes and fried fresh field mushrooms. He showed us the potatoes the dirt still on them a basket of mushrooms freshly picked trout swimming in an old metal drum a cast iron skillet and yes I thought why would we want to go back and eat Gary's slops the warm fire flickering in the yard.

Terry gave us each an old milk crate to sit on then he went back behind the partition wall and came out with two cleanskin bottles of wine. He took the cap off one put the other down beside him and poured us all a glass. He sat down on the other crate. Well boys he said here's to the upper classes god bless them all and may they live forever which obviously was a strange thing to say. It wasn't until he had been talking for a while scrubbing the potatoes and wrapping them in foil a knob of butter and torn herbs in each that he explained to us how the boss who owned the property his employer had gone into hospital very crook and how he didn't have much longer to live. Last week when he went to see him said Terry the eldest son an arrogant prick told him this was not a good time which was another way of saying piss off we don't want you here. But I've worked for the boss since I left school said Terry and if the eldest son is going to treat me like that what's going to happen to me now? I've put my heart and soul into this place he said. Head Chef can strut around like a cocky on a perch but if it wasn't for the boss there'd be no Cook School and you kids'd still be on the streets.

There was a noise from behind the partition a tap going on then the sound of Rose singing to the radio. Hunter and me didn't know what to say but then the Huntsman raised his glass too. Here's to the upper classes he said whose arses I am privileged to kiss! Terry laughed his head off at that I couldn't help laughing too it was true what would we be without rich people to cook our fine dining for we were going to owe our careers to them. To the upper classes! I said and we all drank together and laughed.

After the potatoes were in the fire Terry showed us around. He lived in the shed behind the partition wall where he'd built himself a little apartment a single bed a cupboard with drawers a radio a sink a bar fridge a kettle a bare light bulb in the masonite ceiling. Rose was at the sink finishing the morning dishes it was crowded in there we had to brush past her on the way. She smiled her half-smile took off her gloves rolled down her sleeves and kissed her dad on the cheek. Before she went out she tried smiling again and this time it was warm. Everyone went quiet for a bit till we heard the car start up and drive away.

Terry explained how he was separated from his wife she'd had an affair with a truck driver but he didn't care he still had Rose that was the main thing Rosie didn't like the truck driver. After she moved out of home she lived for a while with an older fella and they ended up having a kid but this bloke was hitting her so Terry helped her get a little place of her own a one bedroom unit self-contained. His eyes were glazing over now he took off his cap rubbed his bald head his hair all stuck down on one side. I asked could we do anything we both felt stupid now. I'm all right he said life's a bitch. He wiped his eyes and put his cap back on. Come on he said let's eat.

He took a landing net off the wall of the shed netted three trout from the drum then whacked each one on the head with a stick and gave me a long bendy filleting knife to gut them. Hunter got a paring knife to stalk and peel the mushrooms. Terry stuffed the trout with butter and thyme wrapped them in foil and laid them on the coals the mushrooms he fried with butter and tarragon and well let me tell you the meal we ate then was as good as anything I ever tasted.

After we finished I picked up my glass and moved away from the fire out into the yard past where the last of the orange light was flickering on the gravel all the stars out the moon hardly risen. Well here's a crossroads I thought. I'd been reading about peasant food rustic they called it and here it was a celebration of what the earth has given. But I didn't want to be a peasant I wanted to be the man who could destroy a suit. Who is Terry I thought is he our equal no he's our supplier he's there to serve us we cultivate a friendship for one purpose. The lamb in the pen is what connects me to Terry the reason to have him as my friend. That's cruel thinking I know but if I'm going to crawl out of the swamp and climb my way up cruel thinking is what I need.

Me and Hunter went out to Terry's pretty well every night after that no-one missed us no-one cared. Sometimes Rose was there. Gary didn't care that was two meals less he had to cook and Fabian after five he disappeared into the house and we never saw him again till morning. I was always down the shed straight after class every afternoon to have a look at my lamb it knew me now it knew I was coming I could hear it bleating when I came round the track. Terry got barley for me every week from a local stockfeed supplies and helped me rig up a feeder and water trough. I had no trouble getting the grain into my little lamb it woofed it down every morning it got no other feed and after two weeks it had put on nearly seven kilos.

One Saturday night late coming back from Terry's there was a light on in the kitchen. Me and Hunter could hear Fabian's voice so we sneaked around the garden side up under the window to look. Inside were three kids lined up along the wall they were in trouble for sure. One was Lachlan with the spiky hair then Daniel the drughead and last the fat kid Josh. Fabian was paying out on them. They only had a few days left to show they understood the word discipline he was saying and if they couldn't he would tell their parents or social workers or in the case of Daniel his parole officer to come and collect them first thing Monday morning and they would be sent away not with a certificate or a reference but a kick up the arse. He took a soup ladle from a hook and stood in front of Lachlan held the ladle in front of his eyes then dropped it on the floor. Pick it up said Fabian. Lachlan picked it up and handed it back. Your ladle Chef said Fabian. Your ladle Chef said Lachlan. Me and Hunter watched while one by one Fabian dropped the ladle in front of them and one by one they picked it up and said your ladle Chef.

Next thing after that Fabian handed the ladle to Lachlan and pointed to Josh and said hit him. Lachlan was confused so was Josh. Hit him we heard Fabian say. Hit him on the head and say more salt in the sauce. Lachlan was crying now and having trouble getting the words out but he did hit Josh on the head with the soup ladle and he did say more salt in the sauce. Good said Fabian now do it again. Now Josh was crying but that didn't matter Lachlan hit him again and said more salt in the sauce. Now Fabian took the soup ladle off Lachlan who was really shaking and gave it to Josh who was really blubbering and said now hit him meaning Daniel and tell him more salt in the sauce.

Well you get the idea. Daniel I don't think had any tears it was hard to imagine how he could with those eyes but he was rattled that's for sure like one of those dogs that doesn't know whether they are meant to sit or beg. The ladle eventually ended up back with Josh and Fabian said all right give it to me. When Fabian turned around to put the soup ladle back on the hook we both had to duck down quick. We heard Fabian giving them one last bawling out how this was an opportunity that only came around once in a lifetime and how Head Chef and his TV crew were coming and this humiliation would be nothing to the humiliation they'd feel if they kept cooking crap. When we moved back around the far side of the garden we saw the three of them filing out their tails between their legs. A little while after that Fabian came out turned the light off and shut the door. Hunter didn't make any jokes.

Two days after that it was official Fabian said Head Chef and his crew were coming next Monday one week from today. Look sharp people I don't want any passengers he said. I increased my lamb's ration feeding it up to three times a day morning lunch and evening. Now it was not so piggish I got Hunter to hold it down and pull its mouth open while I shoved the grain in a handful at a time and washed it down with the hose. In those last two days my lamb put on two more kilos and was just about ready for slaughter.

Grain-fed lamb rack with a rosemary and red wine *jus* minted fresh peas and baby kipfler potatoes the peas and potatoes I would pick early the lamb Terry would slaughter the Friday before so I could hang it over the weekend. I probably overdid the force-feeding a bit during those last few days and by Friday my lamb was looking a bit glassy-eyed. I gave it no food and plenty of water and left it with Terry saying I would be back after morning classes to check but when I went back at lunchtime Terry had already slaughtered it and had it hanging skinned on the frame. It was a bummer I missed it. He said it had got worse during the morning and by eleven o'clock it was lying in the corner of its pen not moving at all. But don't worry said Terry it's good meat all right you've done well he pinched the flesh and with his knife he cut into it a little slice at an angle near the rump. It was very bright and pink. Terry hung it that afternoon in the coolroom tenderstretch a stainless steel mixing bowl underneath to catch the drips and after lunch the whole class including Fabian stopped to watch when he shouldered it in. I wrote my name on a piece of paper and pinned it to my lamb and I don't mind saying that in that moment I felt as proud as punch.

I was up at dawn that Monday frost on the ground a fog that wouldn't lift picking my mint and peas pulling up my potatoes putting them all in the coolroom. Before class Fabian helped me butcher my lamb breaking it down till I had one beautiful-looking best end rack trimmed and chined the meat marbled pale pink juicy and tender to the touch I had done what no-one else had done I could see Fabian was impressed. He spent the whole class looking at the door listening for the Audi at ten-thirty he told us to break. We watched him hurry back over to the house and when he came back he had that steely look in his eye. Head Chef won't be coming today he said he has been delayed he will be here next Monday but let's not let that spoil our day he said we will prep cook and plate our dishes for lunch then we will taste and discuss. We did what Fabian said but no way the day wasn't spoiled. I didn't care what my classmates thought I was cooking for Head Chef.

Straightaway at the end of class I went and saw Terry and got him to get me another lamb. If Head Chef turned up next Monday I would need to be ready again. There was no way this second lamb could be anywhere near as good as the first but what could I do I shoved barley and lupins into it like berley into a sock.

But Head Chef didn't turn up next Monday or the Monday after that. Every morning first thing I would go out to feed my lambs every evening me and Hunter would eat and drink with Terry down the shed. There was no Head Chef to impress but still every day I was learning. Three grain-fed lambs reared and slaughtered twenty maybe thirty different lamb dishes prepped and cooked every method different different cut different accompaniment every time. I'd learnt nearly all there was to know about getting top-quality meat on the plate the feed proportions protein content fat outcomes skin thickness how to finish and turn them out ready for slaughter. I'd experimented with additives too the last a generous amount of fresh rosemary in the final feed and the lamb bottle-fed three-to-one pinot noir and water.

I was working on my vegetables too. If my lamb had been hung say only the day before Head Chef arrived and was a bit tough I would need to plan for a slow-cooked dish a braised shoulder maybe in a good stock with vegetables and herbs. But if my slaughtered lamb had already been hung for a week with my next lamb still a day away from being finished I would only want to grill it for a minute or two each side say a good loin cut with seasonal greens. Back in late March when I first started planning my dish there were peas and beans every-where shelling snap snow dwarf climbing scarlet runner and my lamb would be served with these a rack maybe with fresh minted peas or a chargrilled rump with buttered beans. Right up to the end of April the tomato bushes were loaded I knew I could do a nice *niçoise* with cherry tomatoes and olives or a homely Italian pot with romas rosemary and red wine but then the tomatoes started falling from the bushes and Fabian was teaching us how to make *sugo*. Autumn and the mush-rooms were popping up everywhere out on the paddocks I could have done a nice slow-braised leg with garlic whole shallots field mushrooms and thyme but trouble was again Head Chef didn't come and the mushrooms turned to mush. Now it was midwinter.

I was sure Head Chef was coming but the others weren't they said Fabian was just keeping us on our toes training us up ready for that crazy hour before service. Hunna being Hunna says no there are cameras everywhere we *are* the show they've been watching us from the start. Hunna. Three more kids left during that time one of them Daniel the drughead. He got into a fight one day in the kitchen and when this other kid went at him from behind to try and get the knife he knocked a pan of hot oil off the stove and it went all down this kid's leg and he started jumping and screaming. Fabian ran cold water over it and took him off to hospital but the kid who had been fighting Daniel in the first place couldn't help himself. He kept giving it to him all afternoon saying how he'd sent that kid to hospital until Daniel went off his nut and that kid went to hospital too. The next day a guy in a suit came to pick Daniel up and take him away. The other kids didn't come back either.

Stay ready I told myself stay focussed know what you have to do. We are here to serve we are servants in the service industry through service we exult ourselves. Was there ever any culture anywhere in history that didn't have its slaves who do you think built the pyramids the pharaohs? All those counsellors they always said my anger and all my bad things were because of my shame who I was where I came from how I had to get myself off the bottom one rung only a factory job a pay packet once a week but they were wrong. That's why they could never fix me. Shame is my engine. I am not going to run from it I am going to nurture and love it. I am going to make every mistake hurt.

When Dad got sick forty years of age a young man really his whole life ahead of him working in that place breathing that stuff since the day he left school what did he have at the end nothing. A week's wage direct deposited super extracted enough to keep his head above water and call himself a working man without shame. I don't want to work for a boss who props me up just above drowning I want to work for a customer who knows I am below them and who knows that I know. This is my shame it is a shame I want to be proud of. The money is elsewhere it's always been elsewhere that is the truth of our lives someone else somewhere above is holding the string dangling it in front of our eyes do we jump like dogs for a treat and try to grab our little handful or do we flatten our ears say I'm your dog you're my master give him shame out of every pore make him feel so big and special that he can't help dropping something down for you. It's not up to us to change them our job is to lick their boots kiss their arses let them make the money they're the ones who know how to and let's be thankful for what trickles down.

I split the big pen into four smaller pens so I could rotate my lambs like vegetables in pen four a grain-fed lamb a day or two away from slaughter in pen one a fresh lamb just in from the paddock. When the lamb in pen four came on it would be killed and hung and all the lambs moved up a pen the slaughtered lamb left in the coolroom till it was clear Head Chef wasn't coming then butchered like the others. The good cuts I'd put aside for practice the cheap cuts I gave to Gary the bones I used for stock. I'd made myself a special set of knives that I kept wrapped in an old red tea-towel. I did all the killing and cutting myself.

Anyway after all that with everyone thinking no way Head Chef was ever coming back last Friday after lunch Fabian came into the kitchen all pale-faced and shaking and said he was coming that night. He was going to have guests with him VIPs Fabian said and they would need a full three-course menu three entrées three mains three desserts. End of playtime said Fabian five months at Cook School and our judgment was at hand.

Well as you can imagine no time for dithering then we snapped into action pretty quick. Head Chef plus three guests we would be cooking for four the first course to be served at six-thirty sharp. Me Hunter and Josh would be Fabian's Chefs de Partie me on meat Hunter on chicken Josh on pastry Fabian on fish. He put a Commis Chef below each of us and made the last guy waiter that's nine in all and for the next four and half hours we prepared ourselves for battle.

I had one lamb slaughtered and hanging five days and one in pen four still two days off being finished I decided to use the one already slaughtered. For vegetables I went out to the garden my best bet now baby carrots and some pink fur apple potatoes very waxy pale-pink skin I could do them parboiled with butter and parsley. My main green I decided would be spinach sautéed with garlic finished with a squeeze of lemon and with this I'd do a boned shoulder of lamb rolled with herb stuffing and for entrée a single loin cutlet like Head Chef had done that day when he ruined his suit moist and pink and topped with my own *jus* reduced from the lamb stock I had going served with French-cut deep-fried Jerusalem artichokes and a sorrel garnish. Hunter was doing *saltimbocca* and for entrée a grilled stuffed quail.

After we had planned our dishes which took nearly an hour Fabian took us inside. This was the first time any of us had ever been in the house it was a weird experience. We could see the big inground swimming pool kids' playthings scattered around a big wooden table and chairs on a deck under a pergola. He took us through the sliding glass doors into an open-plan kitchen very modern big windows looking out onto the yard. Fabian's breakfast dishes were still on the bench a bowl and spoon a plate with a half-eaten piece of toast and on the table over in the corner by the window a pile of newspapers a bottle of red wine an empty glass and a big ashtray full of butts. All right said Fabian we'll prep and cook all our meals in the big kitchen and use this kitchen as a staging post and you he was pointing to the kid who was going to be our waiter Liam a short guy with a baby face a terrible cook. *Oui* Chef said Liam. Our chefs said Fabian will bring the plates over and put them here and you will take them from here into the dining room is that clear? He took us into the dining room a big room with a massive old timber table in the middle a cabinet on the wall with old fashioned plates and cups on another wall a big painting of cows in a field the sky a false-looking blue. This is where our guests will eat said Fabian you could see he never ate in here there was a layer of dust on the table and a stale musty smell. He showed Liam what he called the humble spot one step back and off to one side and we all watched while Liam practised then we left him there to clean up while we went back to the kitchen.

Now a boned shoulder is a bit of an old-fashioned cut but as soon as I had the shoulder off the lamb that had been hanging I knew it was going to taste like nothing no-one had ever tasted. I took off the foreshank and trimmed the shoulder you could smell the rosemary and wine very strong and asked Fabian could he help bone it for me. He was doing a whole baked trout with a fennel *gratin* and for entrée smoked trout *quenelles*. My stuffing would be breadcrumbs pounded garlic lemon zest a bit of thyme bound with a fresh egg the boned shoulder spread with this then rolled and tied and left to stand at room temperature for forty-five minutes before being browned on a griddle and slow roasted in a moderate oven then rested and carved a beautiful spiral of pink meat and stuffing. With my lamb butchered and my cuts laid out ready at my station and my Commis Chef an acne-faced kid called Jacob grating bread for breadcrumbs I went outside into the garden.

It was one of those classic winter days the morning drizzle lifting about eleven and after that all day a blue sky and a chill which now about four got chillier. There were a few kids out in the garden collecting what their chefs had told them all underlings I probably should have sent my underling out too but I wanted to choose my ingredients myself this is what real chefs do. I got the vegetables and herbs back inside and got my team working on them everyone was working quiet and steady hardly any talk the vegies prepped the stuffing made the shoulder stuffed and rolled my *jus* reducing on the stove. I looked at Fabian he looked more worried than any of us his Commis Chef Christian was doing the *quenelles* Fabian had his mind on other things.

By five-thirty my shoulder was browned and in the oven and all the vegetables prepped. A few of the kids including my Commis Chef were called in to help set the table so I stood at my station for a while to see if I'd covered everything and that's when I remembered the lemon. It was a tiny thing half a teaspoon of zest in the stuffing too late for that and a squeeze of juice on the spinach but I had to have it. Where are you going? Hunter said. I told him and asked him to watch my oven and when Jacob my Commis Chef came back to get the water on for the potatoes. Huntsman smiled he looked happy distant toothpicking his *saltimbocca* like he was already some-where else.

Outside still in my apron I was sneaking along the garden fence towards the orchard when behind me I heard the Audi pull up and saw the glow of the headlights on the house. I watched Head Chef get out I could see him clearly he was wearing a suit talking on his mobile a silver car pulled up behind and another guy in a suit got out. Head Chef shook this guy's hand I could see them talking Head Chef pointing here and there around the farm. Next a taxi pulled up and three people got out. Everyone shook everyone's hand and after a bit more talk the guy with the silver car got in and drove away. Head Chef and the others walked up to the house.

The cool night air was coming down a fog already on the hill I crept past the chickens hushing them as I went then out the end of the compound into the orchard. It was very misty now the light white and all quiet and still. The lemons were way over there on the far side of the orchard the citrus section lemons limes oranges mandarins grapefruit all two by two in rows. It felt strange there deep in the orchard among the trees and no-one else around but when I got closer I thought I heard a radio going a DJ's voice and the start of a song. At first I thought maybe it was Terry in the shed getting dinner ready but then I realised it was coming from inside the orchard.

It was Rose. She was loading the branches she'd pruned onto a tractor trailer. I didn't know what to do. She had a beanie on and was wearing her dad's old puffy jacket the shoulders shimmering in the light. Of course I wanted to see her out here all alone with the sky nearly dark I would have to pass her to get to the lemons but trouble was I had business back at the kitchen I had to get my citrus and get out. She saw me coming she had an armful of branches I was passing a couple of rows away I could hardly pretend I wasn't there. Hello I said. Rose put her load in the trailer.

What are you doing out here? she asked. Getting a lemon I said. For some reason she thought that was funny. I couldn't help it I had started a conversation now I didn't know how to stop. And are you the one who said my dad should kick my boyfriend out of the flat he said you were a know-all type. I didn't know what to say. No I said I wouldn't have said that why would I it's not up to me to say things like that. Rose didn't answer she threw another pile of branches onto the trailer. We haven't seen you around for a while I said. I stepped through the gap in the trees till I was standing opposite. I think your dad misses you I said he hasn't been happy. But Rose didn't answer.

Are you back to stay? I asked. I don't think anyone can be happy said Rose when they're expected to do that much killing. Now she was looking straight at me I was looking at her lips. What do you want the lemon for? she asked. I thought it might be a trick question. Sautéed spinach with garlic I said I'm serving it alongside a stuffed shoulder of lamb baby carrots and pink fur apple potatoes with a butter and garlic sauce maybe I could cook for you one night? I don't know where that came from it just came out of my mouth. That would be nice she said Nathan hand Mummy the secateurs. And that's when I realised there was a kid sitting up on the front seat of the tractor a little kid about three or four Terry said she had a kid. He handed down the secateurs and Rose started clipping some branches.

You should get your lemon she said. Obviously I should get my lemon but I couldn't get my feet to move. I was thinking about Kelly she used to live across the road and how we did it that time in her room my first time my only time her parents were out it was all over in five minutes. She wanted to be a hairdresser I bet she's not I bet she married a dropkick a kid on each hip. Rose kept looking at me I never realised how sad she looked. There was a loud noise from the house a car door slamming. Rose climbed up onto the tractor alongside her kid. She started the engine turned the headlights on and putt-putted off between the rows back towards the shed.

It was the very last of the light and the lemons when I found them were almost glowing. I picked one and hurried back to the kitchen when I got there everything was chaos. Fabian and Liam the waiter were coming out the gate struggling with one end each of the big wooden dining table. I asked Hunter what was going on. Head Chef and his three guests he said were already inside the house drinking but they didn't want to dine in there they wanted to dine in the kitchen so they could be close to the action. We're going to set the table up at the far end near Gary's station we have to cook and serve while they watch.

Fabian led the way through the door bumping and bashing the table turning it on its side to get it through. He was a wreck. His face was all red he was sweating and shouting instructions to his Commis Chef to turn the oil down and to everyone in the kitchen to hold fire until they got the table set up and had the guests seated. He and Liam pushed the work benches back against the wall at the servery end and set the table up there. Liam ran back and forth to the house for the chairs the tablecloth the cutlery the flowers and started setting the table again. I was working as fast as I could I was in the zone I could feel a little of the orchard conversation clinging to me the steps I'd rehearsed would have to be changed I was flying by the seat of my pants but somehow everything was all right.

My Commis Chef Jacob had done what I'd told him the carrots blanched potatoes parboiled the Jerusalem artichokes cut ready for frying the cutlets waiting they would be grilled at the last minute but the trouble was the roast. It had been in the oven nearly an hour. I needed to cover and rest it before serving but if I took it out and covered and rested it now by the time the main course was served my roast would be cold. I decided to do a second. The guests were still in the house drinking their aperitifs Liam still setting the table I calculated by the time they were seated given menus served first course the dishes taken away drinks served again I could have my second roast rolled stuffed browned baked rested and carved and ready to go to the table. I ran to the coolroom got down my lamb made a temporary bench unrolled my red teatowel and butchered and boned my second shoulder doing exactly what I'd watched Fabian do while Jacob made another stuffing.

When I came back out of the coolroom the dinner guests had arrived Head Chef and two Asian guys both in dark snappy suits and another guy tanned and blond a powder-blue suit he looked like he'd just flown down from Byron. With his guests following Head Chef started wandering around inspecting what everyone was doing making suggestions explaining things to his friends dipping his finger in the sauce. You could feel the tension. When they passed my station I didn't look up I was stuffing and rolling my lamb. You're cutting it fine said Head Chef.

After intimidating everyone for a while Head Chef called Liam over to the table. Liam listened with his head bowed then with a frightened look at Fabian he ran back to the house. After a while he came back with two bottles of wine one red one white and started taking orders.

So that was prep now service. For entrée two of the guests ordered Fabian's *quenelles* one Hunter's quail and Head Chef my lamb loin cutlet. By the time it was on the table I was already working to get my roast ready two people had ordered it but I made sure I looked over when Head Chef started eating and I knew straightaway all my work from way back when was it in March had with that one bite paid off. I'm not going to say his eyes rolled back in his head and his tongue fell out of his mouth that would be an exaggeration but close. My roast was good too despite the rush the meat very tender and succulent when you slid the knife through the colour and smell just right. Liam was working his arse off now running backwards and forwards they were drinking a lot of wine. It was strange us scraping the plates and starting the washing up with the four of them still sitting at the table in full view drinking and talking but after the last plate was cleared and Josh's *tartes aux pommes* were served Head Chef stood up with his wine glass raised and got the others up too. Congratulations to you all he said you have served a wonderful meal! It wasn't until he'd sat back down and was leaning over talking very hushed to his friends that I noticed Fabian at the station beside me with a plate of baked trout barely eaten. Head Chef had ordered the baked trout.

It was all quiet in the kitchen then just the hubbub of talk from the table we could hear the occasional phrase they were talking about business now the food just a lingering smell in the room. After about an hour the guests strolled back over to the house the kitchen was cleaned the things put away the table and chairs taken back and we all sat down to eat.

The talking and drinking went on in the house for a long while after that we all went to bed about ten. Me and Hunter talked for a bit very quiet on our bunks it was hard to know what the others were thinking they were either asleep or had their earbuds in. Hunter said that was humiliating having them there in the kitchen like that and us their performing monkeys I said yes we were performing what's wrong with that food is theatre why hide it away? But Hunna had gone all huffy now I reckon it was because his *saltimbocca* was overcooked.

Me I lay awake for a long while till I remembered

something funny. I was at the circus Mum and Dad took me it was on the footy ground past the shopping centre next to the paddocks I must have been about five. There were elephants and horses trapeze artists all that. But what I remembered now was the clown act all these clowns dressed as chefs white uniforms and hats and each a wooden spoon. One chef started chasing one of the other chefs with his spoon trying to hit him on the head. And that chef started chasing a different chef who started chasing a different chef again and so on a whole line of them until the one who'd got hit first caught up with the end of the line so the line turned into a circle and all the chefs were hitting each other around and around so you didn't know who was the first one to get hit or who hit him and you know sometimes I think that's how it is.

I'd just fallen asleep after thinking about this when the next thing I know there's a torch in my face and Fabian is above me saying *get up get up*. Hunter was already up pulling on his jumper. They want us at the house he said. They want more food said Fabian Head Chef has asked for you two especially. Hurry he said they're waiting. The other kids were all waking up now turning on their bedside lamps asking what's going on? They watched from their bunks while we followed Fabian out the door. He wants offal said Fabian a chef always wants offal when he's trying to impress. Me and Hunter were having trouble following him skipping along behind still half-asleep and him taking big strides like someone on their way to put out a fire. One of the great mysteries boys he was saying but in a whisper of culinary culture is how you can flatter someone's ego with a serving of guts on a plate. We were crossing the gravel all the lights on in the house in the big kitchen too very bright and clean the stainless steel sparkling and now here we were about to mess it up again. Fabian stood behind one of the benches and gave us our instructions.

All right he said now listen two more guests have just arrived he wants supper for six offal dishes only I've picked out some things we can do quickly the ingredients are up on the board. We are going to have to work fast said Fabian and as a team. First dish he said pointing is grilled trout roe with butter and lemon not offal strictly but it'll do I'll get the fish and do that myself then next chicken liver *brochettes* Hunter livers grilled on skewers you will need six chickens and you he said looking at me lambs' brains *au beurre noisette* do you still have the head? It was all going very fast Hunna was still in his pyjama pants I was still half-asleep he meant the head of the lamb I'd butchered. I still had the head but I'd smashed it up and put it in the bucket for stock bones and as for the brains I was telling all this to Fabian I'd chucked them out in the rubbish. Fabian really wanted to give me a lecture now about how we respect the animal by using every part but there wasn't enough time for that. Go and get another head he said. No get another two. And you he said to Hunter when you've got your pants on go and kill six chickens.

I went back to the bunkhouse and got my torch. While Hunter went to the chicken coop I went back to the orchard it was dark and eerie no moon except a skinny banana I stuffed my pockets with lemons. The track to the shed was slippery from yesterday's showers when I got there I could see a light on behind the partition. What am I doing I thought what will Rose think of me out here with my torch at midnight come to slaughter the lambs?

What do you want Terry said behind me I had no idea where he'd come from he was holding a small paper bag. Head

Chef is here I said he's brought guests and now two more have arrived where have you been all day my lamb shoulder was superb. They need more food up at the house I said I smashed the head for stock bones I need two lambs we're doing brains *au beurre noisette*. It was hard to tell if he was listening I turned around and saw Rose in the partition doorway with her kid in his Spiderman pyjamas clinging to her like a koala. The little fella's sick said Terry he's got a fever I can't help you now.

Can I have your knife though I said your killing knife I need to kill two lambs. Rose wouldn't look at me the loser come to kill the lambs the little kid turned his head though and did. I'm sorry Rose I said I'm really sorry but Head Chef's up there with his guests and they want brains for supper. I used the other head for stock bones and threw the brains away I'll be quick I promise and quiet. Rose went back inside she didn't look at me or speak. Terry you understand don't you I said it's like with the boss you've got to make him happy we have to grovel it's what we do. Terry was staring off into the distance like he had someone else more important talking to him and I was a yapping dog. It's in the pouch on the bench he said then he went inside.

I got Terry's knife and sharpening steel out of the pouch ran the steel a few times down the knife and tested the edge with my thumb. I could hear the kid crying Rose trying to give it the medicine it was hard to concentrate with that noise let alone the music coming from the house Jamiroquai again they must have had the back door open smoking cigarettes there was a mad squawking coming from the chookpen too. The slaughter was nowhere near as clean as Terry's the first lamb from pen four especially bucked and struggled like it had too much time to think I wonder if the moment turned out like it thought? It was a struggle to get it down onto the ground let alone get its neck over the dish but anyway I won't go into it after a while I was walking back to the kitchen carrying two lambs' heads by the ears in the shed behind me hanging side by side on a rope tied to the rafters the carcasses for another day.

The chookpen when I passed it had a cloud of feathers Hunter struggling with his last chook which without a head refused to die the other five already headless stacked in a pile on the bench by the gate. We were both covered in blood. Come on hurry I said to Hunter just whack it on the fence post. I didn't wait to see if he did I was already back at the kitchen where Fabian was waiting ready to add a new dish *cervelle au beurre noisette* to my repertoire.

Fabian had already milked his trout six roe lined up on a plate he looked at me when I came in blood all up my arms and my two lambs' heads hanging down. Use a cleaver he said split them open. I put them on the bench and got a cleaver and with a sharp whack I cracked open the skulls and wrenched them apart with my fingers. The brains inside were still warm and slippery I slid them out onto the bench. Hunter came in with an armful of headless chickens he didn't look happy and for a long while after that it was all quiet while I prepped my brains and helped Hunter dissect his chickens and pluck the livers out.

Brains should be soaked before you poach them and poached before you fry but I had no time to soak. I poached them in a *court bouillon* removed the membranes and pressed them for a while under a board and heavy pot. Soon we were all quick-frying our dishes Fabian his roe Hunter his livers me my brains all up from slaughter to table in less than fifty minutes. We plated up I garnished mine with warm baby onions caramelised in balsamic and some sprigs of fresh Italian parsley. All right said Fabian you serve I'll clean up remember dishes in the centre clean plates knives and forks fresh water in the jug and fresh wine glasses for all it will be over soon. It was odd that last thing he said I couldn't help thinking about it when me and Hunter crossed the gravel between the kitchen and the house me carrying the brains and trout roe Hunter his chicken liver *brochettes*. I could see Josh the fat kid in his pyjamas standing outside the bunkhouse watching. When we came in through the back door into the kitchen it was a mess empty wine bottles everywhere the smell of cigarettes we looked at each other going into the lions' den two no-hopers from nowhere about to serve the VIPs. I smiled but Hunna had a grim look like he wanted to be somewhere else.

The two new guests were ladies let me put it that way both dressed up with lots of make-up perfume and hair. One was sitting on the tanned Aussie guy's lap the other was slow dancing in the corner with an Asian guy watching. Head Chef and the other Asian guy were talking at one end of the table their noses almost touching but as soon as we came in carrying our dishes Head Chef stood up his arms out wide he was very pissed. Ladies and gentlemen he said supper is served boys put them there clear the table bring fresh cutlery and plates! We put the dishes on the table. As soon as we did Head Chef picked one of Hunter's livers off its skewer and popped it theatrically in his mouth. He chewed and nodded it was hard to tell what this nod was saying. More wine boys he said more wine there are two reds on the bottom shelf in the pantry fresh glasses fresh glasses come on everyone sit down and enjoy!

Well what can I say about that night. After all that time wondering if Head Chef would ever come back and if he did would I please him and if I pleased him how would I know and here I was serving him at his table. Huntsman couldn't handle it he'd lost his sense of humour that's for sure. I said get over it don't kid yourself cooking is learning how to do what you're told. No he said cooking is self-expression if I want to be a slave I'll work in a factory like my dad and his dad before him. He was being a dickhead all right. I got him to help me re-set the table and serve the wine then after that he said he was going. Go I said I was way past caring about Hunter and his hurt little ego it wouldn't be Hunter who Head Chef remembered next morning it wouldn't be Hunter he put in his phone.

The two Asian guys were investors the tanned Aussie guy Head Chef's business partner and from what I could make out they were trying to get the Asians to invest in their new Singapore venture. It was hard to follow everything I was in and out of the kitchen clearing dishes pouring wine about two in the morning I even went back to the big kitchen to warm up the rest of my roast one of the Asian guys liked it so much. Of course of course! said Head Chef.

In the big kitchen I found Fabian on his own sitting at one of the benches by the window drinking. It's going well I said. When I got back to the house Head Chef was standing up at the head of the table talking about Cook School and how he'd set it up all the students hand-picked troubled kids intensely trained under his strict supervision many of them young ladies he said smiling and not ugly ones either. The other guys were laughing at this I sort of laughed too it wasn't true how could it be but Head Chef was doing business and business isn't about being true he was there to make his investors happy and if that meant offering them pretty young chefs well that was all right wasn't it? Head Chef saw me laughing it was not a big laugh just a small one and the next thing I know he's asking what's your ambition boy? Even the ladies were looking at me now no-one had ever asked me a question like that before not with the word ambition anyway. What's your ambition boy? I hadn't answered yet I wasn't sure I knew how. To be a chef like you Chef I said and run a restaurant of my own the best food possible from the best ingredients cooked with love. Head Chef smiled I was a good boy that was the right answer. Bravo he said and he clapped his hands the other guys even the ladies clapped too. That was a good answer you'd have to admit but the strange thing was it was a true answer I wasn't expecting that.

The party went on in the house till four that's when I heard the taxi arrive to pick the ladies up. When I went back to the big kitchen Fabian's bottle and glass were still on the bench but he was gone it was four-thirty when I went to bed. What's your ambition boy? The windows in the bunkhouse were growing light when I finally fell asleep.

All quiet that morning the blinds drawn in the house and a weird feeling around the place. Head Chef and his guests had left early. Late morning we still hadn't seen Fabian then lunchtime I'm in the kitchen and Hunna comes running in. Quick quick he said.

Terry had found Fabian hanging from a tree in the orchard he'd been hanging there for hours. It hadn't worked the knot had slipped and when he'd kicked away the milk crate he was left leaning against the trunk his feet just touching the ground. When I came out of the kitchen the ambulance guys were carrying him past on a stretcher he was blue his eyes rolling back. The other kids were watching it was hard to believe all right. When the cops arrived they took statements eventually they took a statement from me. I told them the last time I saw him was about two in the morning in the big kitchen drinking and how when I went back later he was gone. They asked did I think he had a reason to kill himself and I said no of course not or not one I could think of anyway. I could have said maybe because his trout was overcooked but that would have been a stupid thing to say.

Next they talked to Terry for a long time then the ambulance left. After that Head Chef arrived jumping out of his car very fast walking around in crazy circles Terry trying to explain everything to him then after that another car a guy in a suit this time carrying a clipboard. He walked over to Head Chef who started pointing here and there then they both went into the house. After that over the next couple of hours four more cars came and went the parents of kids coming to pick them up and take them away. The cops left at lunchtime the inspector guy just after two. Around three I made a light meal and took it over to the house a fillet of fresh-caught rainbow trout wrapped in salted quail skin on a bed of slow-braised fennel in a lemon thyme *consommé*. I figured Head Chef hadn't eaten. Around four I went on my own up the hill. There was a gloom over the whole compound now it was hard to believe how quick things had changed how just yesterday I was getting ready to put my lamb shoulder in the oven and now. Around six Head Chef came out of the house. He stopped for a second out in the driveway and looked around then he got in his car. I watched it get smaller and smaller until it disappeared. Next Gary's Mitsubishi arrived he went into the kitchen came out five minutes later with a box of stuff slammed the boot and drove away. We never saw him again.

Well as you can imagine after that things got pretty quiet around Cook School or Kook School as Hunter likes to call it now. That night we ate leftovers he drank nearly a whole bottle of wine. At one point he got to his feet and raised a toast to Fabian but no-one was very enthusiastic the guy had tried to kill himself there was not much to respect about that.

Hunna had changed we never went up the hill anymore never talked like we used to. To be honest I'm not sure he had it in him to be a real chef you can't be a real chef and have strong opinions he had strong opinions all the time. *Haute cuisine* he said was an old-fashioned thing good for a time when there were kings and princes but not when we are all supposed to be equal. He'd been taking secret lessons from Fabian before Fabian tried to top himself Italian peasant cooking the cooking Fabian's mother had done this was the cooking Hunna wanted to do now. I said well sure you do that but if you want to run a top-class restaurant the smaller it is the less space it takes up on the plate the more you can charge for it that's the way you grow your business food needs to be sneaky not honest. Peasant food is for peasants cooked by peasants a peasant's what you were before surely it's not what you want to *be*? Hunter said I was chasing my tail my grain-fed lamb I had to pay for the grain and put that into the price of the plate but grass costs nothing or next to nothing if you lower your costs you lower your mark-up but your profit remains the same. But people don't want grass-fed lamb I said they want lambs they can rely on the same every time. Your grain-fed lamb is wanker food for wankers said Hunna. You're right I said I'm here at Kook School to learn how to become a wanker I don't want to plate up bold and honest flavours grow apples and peaches with grubs I want to plate slivers of hand-reared flesh with garnishes of baby things.

There were only five of us left now at Cook School and only four cooking and eating together in the kitchen near the house. Hunna had moved down to the shed. Rose was pregnant again you could see the bulge under her shirt I was pretty sure it wasn't the guy who beat her in fact I was pretty sure it was the Hun. All those half-smiles and glances they weren't for me she never looked at me not since that night I killed the lambs it was Hunna making all the moves we were going our separate ways. While he trapped game out on the paddocks rabbits button-quails bronzewing pigeons sometimes coming back with a bagful sometimes with nothing cooking them peasant-style in the wood-fired oven Terry built smooching up to Rose I narrowed my world down controlling everything in it until I was controlling the very molecules of my ingredients. When I wasn't with my animals I was in the kitchen with my meat either from the carcasses I had hanging or the new ones I slaughtered cooking each cut a different way each time and taking notes. I was experimenting with reductions too trying to get the purest flavour out of my ingredients distilling the essence of mint and peas for example down to a few millilitres of green slime so that all you would need to do was smear the edge of your plate with it like the swoosh of a painter's brush. In my kitchen there would be no room for error every stage monitored every outcome designed to generate a high-margin loss-proof return.

My next challenge was *agnelet*. Milk lamb three to four weeks old four to five kilos in weight born in winter raised indoors fed milk only the meat very tender and delicate. I moved my lamb pens closer to the house and made three more for my pregnant ewes each ewe a bit bigger than the next. I got Terry to show me how to spot a pregnant one and the ones I spotted I put in my pens. The trick with *agnelet* is to control the mother how she lives what she eats I fed these mothers quality lucerne up to about three weeks before delivery then intensely fed them a mixture of grain rosemary pinot noir and sea salt after that. This way the unborn lamb could take up via the placenta some of those flavours quite focussed and intense *in utero* then softened after birth when I bottle-fed it on high-fat cow's milk and whisked raw eggs. At slaughter I would have a lamb subtly flavoured with a bit of its mother's old grassiness but overlaid with hints of grain rosemary wine and salt yet exceptionally tender on account of the milk and eggs. The best possible cut of this lamb I would pan fry quickly just a smear of oil no sauces fresh-picked blanched green vegetables on the side something pretty like watercress to finish and served with a pinot noir or maybe just filtered water. This was where I wanted to be I was not going to leave things to chance anymore chance was for nature and nature could not be trusted if I was going to have soul in my cooking it would be a soul I created from scratch like God.

Cook School was my university and I was learning the

things I never learned while I was pissing my future up against the wall. What else are rich and successful people except those who've learnt how to manipulate what's around them a guy dealing in the money market architects designing fancy buildings TV guys making TV shows selling dreams to losers writers and their happy endings. That's what civilisation is I reckon manipulating nature. Fabian was gone there was only one person I had to please and that was Head Chef my life had a purpose and that was to see the pleasure on his face when he came back to Cook School called for dinner and tasted my *agnelet*.

Three weeks after Terry found Fabian lying in his own piss under an apple tree in the orchard with a rope around his neck Fabian not only came back from the dead but came back to take up his position again as Sous Chef at Cook School. It must be hard always playing second fiddle I was not going to do that. He looked terrible his skin all pale he walked with a stoop like someone had whacked him too many times across the back of the head. No-one told us he was coming. I was working in the kitchen one morning when I saw a taxi pull up and Fabian in a coat with a travel bag get out. He settled back into the house but we didn't see him much. I had my first *agnelet* and was too busy to bother.

Its mum had dropped it two weeks before and since then

I'd finished it off with a milk diet slaughtered and hung it in the coolroom and was now playing with the first cuts. My first dish I tried was strip loin done *sous-vide* hot-grilled thirty seconds each side sliced into five mil slivers loosely curled and aligned side by side three to the plate with a chive and garlic crusted *pommes Dauphines* and a garnish of mandolined celeriac and baby red cabbage. I had cooked it three or four times now after-hours sitting up late on a stool at the bench tasting and taking notes. It was never quite what I wanted the meat either too tender or not tender enough and the garnishings never quite right. I did all this quietly on my own I had no desire to give away my secrets so all the more surprising then when one night about eleven I heard a voice asking was it any good?

It was Fabian in a red dressing-gown carrying a bottle of wine. You're in here every night he said it better be good. Fabian poured us each a glass and pulled another stool up to the bench. He had been drinking I guess he was always drinking he was a sad man in many ways. He took a knife and fork and cut a piece of my lamb. No *jus* he said. No *jus* I said. We both looked at each other and smiled. He chewed. It was a long time before he spoke. I could see the bruise on his neck very clear against the white skin. Milk lamb about three weeks old he said did you roast it? Three and a half hours *sous-vide* I said then hot-grilled fast. Fabian took another piece. There's red wine in there he said and rosemary too did you cook it in a *jus*? No *jus*, I said. Very subtle he said like the hint of truffle in an omelette when it's been laid down with the eggs. What is it? he said. I told him. He smiled a faraway smile like someone who had just remembered something that made him laugh a long time ago. He nodded. *In utero* he said. *In utero* I said.

It went quiet between us I wasn't sure I should speak eventually I asked Fabian was Head Chef coming back? Why do you want to know? he asked but very grumpy. Well I said that's why I've been working on my *agnelet* you remember the day with the supermarket chops it all started there. Forget about that said Fabian I didn't know what he meant but I was also afraid he would tell me. Cook from your heart he said cook to please yourself slowly quietly the open kitchen the audience the primping for the cameras these are all shallow ephemeral things you don't want to cook for them. Anyway said Fabian Head Chef might not be back for a while he has business stuff to deal with let's just leave it at that. Is the school in trouble? I asked. Fabian emptied his glass and poured himself another.

Fine dining is a fine thing he said but not all that's fine is forever. The big boss is dead said Fabian I probably shouldn't have told you but do you think the sons are going to want to carry on their father's good works? This property is worth millions said Fabian the houses are coming and here we are teaching *haute cuisine* selectively bred hand-reared high-end livestock tuned to the taste of the wealthy customer who's been told that's how it should taste served up with selectively bred even genetically modified early-picked short-life produce molecularly engineered semi-liquids dusts and powders indulgent cooking for indulgent people can we afford to keep doing that? Head Chef wants fresh ingredients one of everything on hand all the time do you have any idea how much that costs? Terry's been complaining for months he says he needs more help that's why his daughter's here but I don't have the heart to tell him the boss is dead he'll find out soon enough and he'll know what that means. The winds of change are coming said Fabian and when they do it'll be chuck steak and bread and butter pudding you can bet your life on that. He skolled another glass. Anyway he said. He dangled the empty wine glass between the fingers of one hand and grabbed the bottle with the other. He staggered off his stool towards the door. I don't see why I should change just yet I said. Fabian turned around. But you will change son he said.

Of course I thought about what Fabian said that night in the kitchen but in the end I disagreed with most of it. There will always be rich people always and they will always need someone to cook for them. You make complicated high-end labour-intensive dishes *so you can charge top dollar for them* that's what that trail of losers I left behind at home never understood lounging about in their hoodies whinging about the bad hand they got dealt the rich have figured it out create a want forget about needs and charge what you like. All those ignorant heads wandering around back home in that shitkicking brain-numbing suburb lining up at the dole office for whoopee a job in a factory what stuffing dim sims when with a puff of magic smoke they could be charging a hundred dollars minimum for a plate with the same per gram amount of ingredients on it the only difference being theirs are squished into a little ball of shit while mine are sculpted on a field of white served by a good-looking waitress one hand behind her back maybe crossing her fingers against the lie.

Have you ever seen the shadow a shoot of baby Russian kale can throw across a cut of pan-seared pink lamb the deep green of a spinach *purée*? Felt the wild rush of service the opening night nerves the audience the theatre the sheer beauty of all those colours and textures assembled on the plate? Fabian Hunter most of them couldn't handle that night gladiators in front of the emperor but me I want to please my betters right up close to their faces. I want them to smell my desperation because when they smell that my heart swells with pride they have smelt the essence of me.

We spend our whole lives being desperate in some way or other trying to please someone the teacher the duty manager the cop the juvenile justice worker always with secret little gestures and thoughts burrowing into their good books but out there in the kitchen that night with four VIPs asking to be served the desperation was out in the open I can't think of anything more honest and the triumph at the end was something to treasure and once you've felt it well. We don't have kings and queens and princes and lords if we did maybe this country would be a more honest place but no we'd rather live like hypocrites patting ourselves on the back telling ourselves we're all equal we're not I'm sure we never were was the convict getting buggered by the trooper? Give me a good ladder to climb that's what I say don't leave me down here in the cellar show me the rung above where a lord is sitting eating pheasant in his manor and let me serve that lord and hope that some day some of his lordliness rubs off on me and when it does and I'm feeling lordly let me see a prince above and let me go and serve that prince and when I'm feeling nice and princely let me see above me a king. Head Chef is my lord of the manor and when I have served and pleased him I know my prince will be waiting above.

Fabian lasted another week the end was sad that's for sure. He came back all hollowed out no enthusiasm for anything he hardly ever turned up to class. We did what we wanted I'm still not even sure why he came back or why Head Chef let him maybe he had nowhere else to go. One day when I was walking from the kitchen to the bunkhouse I looked over the back fence to the big oak tree and lo and behold from a branch above I saw poor Fabian swinging. He'd made no mistake this time the rope very thick tied to the highest branch it must have been an effort getting it up there he was all pale and stiff he must have been there a while. I didn't know what to do I ran to the shed to get Terry he and Hunter helped me cut him down. They took him away later that day cops and parents and all that again. Well that's it I thought school's over just me and Josh in the bunkhouse and Hunter living down the shed then a few days later out of nowhere Fabian's replacement arrived it was strange I'll explain it all.

Two men in a van came to clean out the house and take away all Fabian's things then next day a flash-looking four-wheel-drive pulled up and that tanned guy from that night in the powder-blue suit who ordered my shoulder got out. He called me and Josh into the kitchen to explain we didn't have a clue. All right he said now come out and give me a hand.

He backed his four-wheel-drive up to the kitchen door and we started unloading the things. Boxes of spices coriander cumin turmeric saffron cardamom cinnamon nutmeg cloves big bags of rice slabs of coconut milk half-a-dozen woks. In white foam boxes we brought in vegetables and herbs bok choy een choy choy sum wong bok gai lum chillies lemongrass coriander Asian basil and mint and lined them all up in the coolroom. A poultryman arrived and unloaded twenty ducks two ducks per cage out on the gravel near the garden. It was all happening very fast and weird too because with Hunter living down the shed and the others gone Cook School was just me and the fat kid now it seemed a bit out of whack.

That afternoon the tanned guy stood in front of the whiteboard in the kitchen with his hands in his pockets all casual and cool and talked while me and Josh took notes. Aspics sweetbreads truffles *quenelles* macaroons ice-cream he said. When the royal consort Catherine de' Medici crossed the Alps in 1533 on her way to the French Court of Henry her future husband and brought with her from the rocky hillsides of Tuscany and the kitchens of the Florentine capital recipes inspired by the new world of Renaissance cooking a great French gastronomic tradition was born. Me and Josh were writing fast. And it is this tradition gentlemen said the tanned guy that we in the restaurant industry today have inherited the Franco–Italian tradition of fine dining. His name was Gavin. He had come to teach us *fusion* European and Asian cooking *fused* together into a new thing not one or the other but both we didn't understand it really.

That is the old world said Gavin pointing now at his drawing of Catherine de' Medici crossing the Alps in a carriage but Asia is the new world that's where the excitement and especially the money is now. He drew a quick map of the world a quick Australia at the bottom. We don't need to look anymore across the seas towards a distant Europe he said drawing first a long arrow then a short one we need only look north to our nearest neighbour Asia and its great culinary traditions which have in truth said Gavin I was writing it all down fast always been the most closely linked geographically and spiritually to what we as a people would become. So isn't it natural he said in a way that made you feel if you didn't think it was natural there might be something wrong with you that the use of Asian recipes ingredients and techniques in combination or *fusion* with our inherited Western traditions might signal a new way forward? Who's the equivalent now asked Gavin of the lords and kings back then in the days of *grande cuisine* it's businessmen isn't it and what businessman is there not flying to Asia every second day to wine and dine his customers so what if only a few years ago he was calling it chink food you've got to move with the times.

Gavin was Head Chef's business partner I knew that he owned three restaurants one in Sydney one in Bali one in Phuket I'd seen his picture in the papers but whether or not Head Chef agreed with him that fusion was the future or whether Gavin was going places Head Chef didn't want to go to or whether Gavin was Head Chef's underling and only doing Head Chef's bidding I couldn't tell. It was a strange week all right I kept my lambs quiet just in case I hadn't finished with Franco–Italian yet. Gavin arrived a bit later each morning and drove back a bit earlier each evening till by the end of the second week he was only here a few hours a day. He never turned up on weekends. In the end we hardly saw him and were left pretty much to ourselves.

My ewe in pen seven was very big now and nearly ready to drop the lamb in pen four almost ready for slaughter. It's good to work the muscles before you give it the knife so every morning early I would take my little pen four lamb out walking through the orchard across the paddocks and back around the other side of the hill. One morning out there a couple of weeks after Gavin arrived I came across Hunter checking his traps. It had been drizzling there was a mist hanging low Hunter barely a shape in the distance then next thing I was standing in front of him. He was holding a dead rabbit by the ears. He looked terrible his clothes all dirty his long hair matted a patchy blond beard a string of birds at his waist. He looked at me with my little lamb and what could he do but make a joke.

Tell me the truth said Hunter did you dob me in to the new teacher? We were sitting on the dry ground under a tree we had to kick away the sheep shit it was drizzling again. No I said what makes you say that? Hunter said he'd had a visit from his parole officer and his parole officer had asked him why he wasn't going to class. Hunter said he was learning how to cook game the traditional Italian way but the parole officer wouldn't buy it. They're coming back to get me soon said Hunna they reckon I've broken my parole. Me and Rose and the kid are going Zac he said I reckon it's all over here.

I told him he was wrong we had a new Sous Chef he was teaching us Asian Asia's the future he should come back to school. Hunter snorted. That's all crap he said next it'll be Middle Eastern or North African or some such shit what happened to cooking from the heart? I showed him my lamb it had its ears up listening. I haven't given up on that I said I'm going to keep doing my lamb until I get it right but you've got to move with the times Hunna we're students we have to listen to our teachers. No we don't said Hunter. He flopped the dead rabbit onto the ground and started cutting it down the middle steam drifting up out of the cut.

Did you know Terry's not been paid for nearly two months he said and the only thing we've got to eat at the shed is what I catch or steal? I've already cleaned out the coolroom where do you think all that stuff went? You wouldn't know you're too busy fattening your babies he said but the days here are numbered Zac the sons are selling. Me and Rose have found a place up in the King Valley it belongs to an old mate of Terry's run-down by the sounds of it but I can fix it up. A few sheep and goats some vegies a little vineyard sangiovese apparently a creek down the back I'll build my own oven we'll live off the land I don't want to be someone else's slave. I told him that was idiot-thinking ridiculous-dreaming we can't work for ourselves until we've earned it and we earn it by working for others but he was already miles away scooping the warm steaming guts out of the rabbit peeling the pelt back up over the head.

With no Hunna around I spent most days now with the fat kid Josh. He hardly ever spoke. I reckon he'd spent a fair bit of time in the kitchen with his mum though he sure knew his way around. He was like one of those fat moles you see in those documentaries making a burrow with its nose. He sat up late every night reading Charmaine Solomon with a penlight torch taped to his beanie and we had breakfast together every morning pancakes scrambled eggs French toast or porridge. We took turns cooking and he hardly said two words the whole time.

I spent most mornings after breakfast mucking around in the garden. My lambs were finished. One morning early I said goodbye to the old world and welcomed in the new herded my three pregnant ewes three spring lambs four weeks twelve weeks eighteen weeks all tied together with a long rope out into the far paddock past the orchard where I slaughtered them one by one then piled them up covered them with branches threw diesel on and burned them. The smell of grilled meat hung around most of the day. So that was it I thought sleeves up it's time to start with the ducks.

A good Peking duck is one bred with a big breast a good even layer of fat between the skin and the carcass so when you roast it the skin comes away nice and crisp you serve that on little pancakes with spring onions and hoi sin sauce. I got half-a-dozen ducks with good-looking breasts and healthy plumage from the dozen left of the twenty the poultryman delivered the others had died and put them in the pen where my lambs had been with some chicken wire to stop them getting out. Same with my lambs I'd have my ducks on rotation staggered so each week more or less there would be a new duck ready for when Head Chef and his TV crew came back. The meal would be Peking Duck the most impressive of all Asian dishes almost as exquisite as my *agnelet* would have been if I'd ever got to serve it a clear soup to start crispy skin with pancakes and last the meat carved at the table served with a simple dish of wok-fried vegetables. To get them right the ducks would be fattened but not too much you don't want that layer of fat too sloppy just a firm foundation for the crispy skin. I got to like my ducks they were funny creatures they got the hang of it eventually each in their own little feeding lot eating the ration I gave them.

The days passed quietly mostly drizzling rain after breakfast every morning I was out in my gumboots feeding my ducks checking their weight mucking around with my vegies and after that reading on my bunk practising chopping Asian style with a cleaver then evenings in the kitchen me cooking the mains Josh the dessert the two of us in the dining room hardly a word an hour at the computer researching recipes then bed. I could see what Gavin was on about how the old world's the slow world the new world's fast we need prep to match lifestyle five minutes kitchen to table that's why Asian's the new cuisine and why *coq au vin* won't cut it anymore but I also felt like Europe was where my soul was when I saw duck I saw *canard à l'orange* not Peking or Szechwan I couldn't help it that's who I am. So aside from doing Asian every day like I was told I also put an hour aside each night to read my Larousse and practise French.

Anyway eventually it was time to cook my duck I'd been

practising on chooks Gavin was going to show us. I told him I had some premium ducks one in particular nice and plump I could see he was impressed. He was an odd one Gavin I could never figure him out tanned Aussie bright cotton shirts mates in Bangkok and Manila and all over but always looking over his shoulder like any minute some great catastrophe was going to whack him from behind. He spent more time checking his messages than he did teaching us how to cook the day he turned up for the Peking Duck lesson he spent half an hour standing with the car door open fiddling with his phone before he came inside.

The prep for Peking Duck is long and complicated I'd been at it since early that morning slaughtering my plumpest duck just after first light plucking it like Terry taught drawing beheading and trussing it then here's the tricky bit separating the skin from the meat by blowing through a little cut in the neck. You tie a piece of string around the neck and dip it in and out of a pot of boiling water then hang it somewhere airy to dry this was what I was doing when Gavin turned up about twelve. Josh was doing sticky black rice with coconut milk shaved palm sugar and roasted sesame seeds.

When Gavin came in all distracted he asked had we prepared and I told him what I'd done with my duck. It was drying in the dining room now I said but I needed to get the marinade on and dry it out again could he help me with that? Gavin said yes of course he could but then out of nowhere he said you people think you're so special don't you you say you want to be chefs but aren't you just here for the holiday? I thought that was a pretty weird thing to say considering how hard I'd been working to please him Head Chef and Fabian before that. No I said I'm not here for a holiday it's not much of a holiday anyway of course I want to be a chef. And do you think there's a future in being a chef? Gavin asked which again I thought was strange what did he expect me to say? Of course I said there's a big future I want to serve good food and make people happy I felt good after I said that. Gavin said he was only asking because Head Chef said I was the one to watch he mentioned me especially but there's a lot of people Gavin said who think they have a future and who pretty soon see they don't. I said I believed I did have a future I had no future before but I was willing to learn to listen to do what I was told I know how to take orders I said isn't that the main thing?

Gavin was even more impressed with that answer so I thought maybe now was a good time to ask why we hadn't seen Head Chef for a while. Gavin went quiet then he was thinking about his answer he started grating the ginger I saw Josh looking over he was waiting too.

This business is for young people and you're still young said Gavin talking to Josh too I'm still pretty young myself only thirty-two. But Head Chef's got a wife and kids now the business isn't everything to him which it's got to be if you're going to succeed it's a twenty-four-seven thing. That's fine said

Gavin mixing the marinade if I had a wife as pretty as her and two cute kids like that I'd be slowing down too selling off what I could while I could still get good money for it.

The other thing he said and I shouldn't be saying this is Head Chef's a *poussin* and truffle man. I don't hold that against him but he's been trying to push out into Asia with traditional French *haute cuisine* and I'm not sure that's what they want. In places like Singapore and Mumbai maybe the upper end of town of course you're going to pull customers with fat wallets and three-piece suits thinking they've just popped down from Whitehall but that's old empire in the new empire our customers are finance IT that sort of thing and sure they want whatever makes them feel rich in Western terms but they also want to say we might have been your third-world slaves once but now we want to be decadent with our money and eat food that's ours you see?

Over the past couple of months I've got to say Head Chef has taken his eye off the ball. There's no way traditional French *haute cuisine* is going to cut it in those places with those customers we've been researching I know I've got more frequent flyer points than any man living. But Head Chef won't be told and if we end up insolvent it's going to be him to blame. I've been talking separately to our investors and I'm telling you fusion is the future. Those finance and IT guys don't want to be decadent Westerners they want to be decadent Futurists already for the Beijing restaurant I've got my architect mate to draw up some plans full-wall plasma screens with black and white Cultural Revolution propaganda films white tablecloths with Wedgwood crockery and Chairman Mao printed table napkins. Fusion menu grilled wild hare with Szechwan pepper and star anise on a bed of jasmine rice or Peking-style duck stuffed with *foie gras* and shaved truffle the waitresses blonde Aussie model types but the maitre d' a classic bowing Chinese. You see?

Are you saying this is not Head Chef's idea to teach Asian? I said. It had only just struck me. Not his idea exactly said Gavin but if he wants to expand into Asia then he's got no choice has he? Gavin scraped the ginger off the grater and made a little pile on the bench. But Cook School is still Head Chef's I asked he's still the boss isn't he? Gavin obviously didn't want to answer that. Listen he said wiping his hands you want to become great and famous chefs it's up to you I've been at the front-line and the Asian expansion's where it's at there's no other blue water left. Fabian knew better than anyone the old empire is finished he just didn't know what to do about it. Being a chef is about being restless said Gavin if you stand still for more than a minute before you know it you'll be cooking at some nice little regional butcher's shop conversion *pot-au-feu* and *plats du jour* crowing about the local produce serving dumpy bourgeois on daytrips from the city. You're only young once gentlemen seize the day.

I remembered all that as best I could not because I

thought Gavin was right necessarily but because the next thing we knew he was gone. I had my marinaded duck hanging in front of the fan in the dining room Gavin was gabbling on about what we'd do next a version with bush tucker berries and lemon myrtle-scented rice when his mobile rang he went outside to talk then me and Josh heard the four-wheel-drive start up and drive away.

That day and the next no sign of Gavin I cooked my duck it was pretty bad the next day Hunter turned up at the kitchen to say goodbye. There were no jokes this time he was a grown-up boy it was all over he said. He was going off with Rose and her kid to make their little piece of paradise. Gavin won't be coming back he said you might as well get out now. Get out where I thought go back home with my tail between my legs for me it was forward to cooking in the palaces of the rich or nothing. No I said I'll be sticking around I'm expecting Head Chef back soon. Hunter had that superior look about him I don't know what he had to feel superior about he and his little white trash family running off to live like peasants in the past. Is Terry going too? I asked. Hunter said no Terry was staying put till he got the money he was owed. There was an awkward pause then. I didn't mention Rose I thought that would be best he got her he had her it was all the same to me. Come back to the shed he said and eat with us tonight we'll make a feast. Come on he said for old times' sake before you go and learn how to penetrate Asia.

When I arrived down the shed that evening Josh was having lasagne on his own Terry was stoking a pit fire while Rose's little boy ran around out in the yard chasing the ball Hunter was kicking. Rose wore a dark green dress her belly big she had to hold it in her hands when she saw me she gave me a faraway smile. There was a long table set up inside the shed an old timber door across two sawhorses a stack of plates in the middle a pile of cutlery. I felt strange of course like the landlord come down to play with his serfs Huntsman the happy bolshevik his biggest ambition now to raise a little brood on a few scrawny hectares in the Valley. Terry poured me a Duralex glass from a four-litre cask of cheap shiraz and asked how the new guy was going. I said Gavin was a good guy he told us how the industry was changing how we needed to look north to Asia because that's where the money was now. Terry asked slow and steady could I let him know he hadn't been paid for a while and maybe ask him to have a word with whoever's running the show? I said sure I would.

The dinner was full of big flavours and bold peasant statements in some restaurants some people would pay good money for that but sitting there at that table that evening eating that food I saw how far I'd come towards refinement. Those big peasant flavours were too big for me they left a taste of takeaways and fat shoppers waddling in the mall. I wanted white crockery microherbs and petals plates that squeaked wine glasses that sang things simmered down to their essence. Once you have tasted refinement you don't go back that's how it was for me. I didn't want greens and browns I wanted white white white and most of all *I didn't want to be one of them.* I wanted no matter how humiliating it might be to prove I was better.

Next day late afternoon I heard the car leaving the horn tooting the kid shouting goodbye. Around five I walked down to the shed. I found Terry already drunk sitting in front of a drum fire staring into the coals. He was not a pretty sight his face all wet with tears his shoulders heaving snot coming out of his nose lifting a cask and squirting the wine straight into his mouth. We're losers he said sack the coach restructure the club get fresh blood doesn't matter losers lose that's that. I sat opposite and took a glass. When I first started working for the boss said Terry straight out of school fifteen years of age I thought I would be working for him for life and funny I suppose I did in the end the boss's life I mean. Losers want nothing Zac except to burrow down into their hole stay quiet do their job go home for the weekend nice and simple but these days everything's changing one minute I'm a factory hand next a storeman then a caretaker farmer next I'm running Kook School get down in your hole make yourself comfortable that's my advice to you.

Terry was really turning on the waterworks now. I said if it was all the same to him I might take up my lamb experiments again spring would be here soon there'd be plenty of new ewes in season I wasn't convinced by all this talk of Asian fusion and anyway it was good for a chef to have a few strings to his bow. Terry just gave me a dumb look and put his head in his hands.

I left him by the fire and headed up along the main track towards the compound. Halfway along I turned off onto the smaller track that led up the hill evening falling August and the sunsets still early a low mist not quite drizzle coming down. I walked to the old spot and looked back. The mist made everything glow it picked up the twilight and spread it on everything and everything very still. I saw Josh coming out of the bunkhouse he was wearing a coat carrying a bag he walked to the front of the house and waited. I could see the back gate open the pigs had broken out of their pen and were rooting around under the oak tree ducks swimming on the green water of the swimming pool and waddling around on the grass. Did Josh let them out? Just then I saw headlights sweeping along the road from the highway. The car pulled up and Josh got in I heard the door slam. A couple of ducks looked up. I watched the car drive away.

I went down to the house the pigs and ducks took no notice of me the door was open everything just how it was after the guys had come to clean out Fabian's things except very musty now and smelly and scary too knowing no-one had been in there. The power was still on the phone had dial tone. I spent a while looking around and finally found what I was looking for in a cupboard under the bench. On top of the phone books a small black book with A to Z pages Head Chef's number exactly where I expected. I dialled a woman answered after I'd started talking I realised it was his wife she was distant at first even a bit rude I told her I was ringing from Cook School that we'd not seen Head Chef for a while and I was wondering when we might expect him back.

She said he wasn't home right now he was away on business would I like her to take a message? I thought that was a pretty nice thing to say considering she didn't know me I gave her my name said it was urgent and asked could Head Chef drop by sometime to clear things up? There was a bit of a pause on the end of the line after that I wasn't sure she'd heard I started repeating myself but she said no it was OK she would pass it on as soon as he got back. I could hear the kids playing in the background. Are you all right in the meantime? she asked which was nice. I told her I was fine I was working hard I thought Head Chef would be pleased and after that we hung up.

When I went outside it was nearly dark so it was hard at first to make out what one of the pigs was doing pushing something up out of the ground with its snout. It was not until this pig actually threw this thing up away out of the shadow of the tree a dark round thing that I realised it was a truffle. I remember Terry said a long time back that's why the tree was planted when the boss first bought the property an ilex oak fifteen years old the mycorrhiza well established.

I shooed the pig away bent down and picked it up and brought it to my nose. I won't try to explain what I smelled no-one has ever been able to all I knew was somewhere in that smell was my future. Gavin was a distraction this was the real thing one shave would be enough to lift my plates into the palaces of kings.

I will start all over again. *Agneau de lait farci.* By the time Head Chef came back to answer my call I'd have it ready a heavily pregnant ewe her milk already down with that milk I'd make a young very soft pecorino-style cheese slaughter the ewe take the *in utero* lamb and slaughter it then draw and stuff it with the cheese made from its mother's milk flavoured with black truffle shavings the whole thing slow-roasted and served in its juices. I could feel my heart pounding. I held the truffle in the palm of my hand went to the kitchen put it in a jar sealed it tight and that night I slept with the jar under my pillow dreaming all kinds of dreams.

The window's open there's a nice cool breeze I'm at my new computer at my new desk in my new room in a house in one of the best suburbs in Melbourne looking out at the tops of the pencil pines and the roof of the house next door. Melody is doing laps in the pool.

Head Chef never did come back I waited a long time all right. One day I got a frantic email from Mum telling me Dad was dead and asking could I come home. At first I said yes but then I thought about it. What if Head Chef came back in the meantime I thought to see what I was up to with my new lamb hanging there dripping into the dish and me not around to cook it? I wrote back and said no. She wrote back pleading. I let the emails pile up till they stopped. I celebrated my nine-teenth birthday with *agneau de lait farci* on my own in the dining room and don't worry it was good.

Then one morning in the kitchen stringing beans I saw a flash car pull up and the driver get out. He had come to pick me up he said and take me into town he told me to get my bag. It was two months since Josh left and just me at the school I could see he was weirded out by all the silence. A clean-cut guy in a tight dark suit his sunglasses pushed back on his head. I looked around everywhere for Terry I hadn't seen him for days even ran down to the shed to try and find him there but by now the driver was beeping. I didn't know why I was saying goodbye but I did. I got in the back seat of the car all bamboozled and we drove down the road to the highway.

An hour and a half later we were in a quiet street outside a high hedge a gate a driveway a big house right down there at the end. I asked the driver did he want money even though I had none but he just waved me away. I got my daypack and got out. I didn't have much a few clothes toiletries my workbook the Larousse my knives my clock my truffle in a jar. The car sat there its motor running the street all dark and shady and cool from the big trees over the road. The driver leaned across and pointed towards the house. Go in he said.

I pushed open the gate. Well let me tell you that driveway when I walked up it felt like the yellow brick road the gravel raked the garden beds neat a gold-plated doorbell a carved wooden door the house so big and me so small what kind of adventure is this? I was just about to ring the bell when the door opened and next thing a man is standing there a middle-aged man wearing a suit carrying a briefcase I could smell his aftershave very strong. Ah! he said you're here I'm Ian go inside. The man walked past me down the steps then down the drive towards the car still waiting in the street. I saw him get in he talked to the driver then the window came down and he flicked his hand at me like he was shooing me away. Go in he said. The car drove away.

The front door was open I took a few steps in. It was a mansion all right you've never seen anything like it you could have fitted our house in the foyer. Now out of a room somewhere a young man about my age good-looking perfect skin a breezy smile started walking across the foyer towards me. You must be the cook he said then over his shoulder Deidre the cook is here! I'm Nick said the young man Melody's boyfriend nice to meet you. The young man went out the front door I could hear him close it behind him. I stood there holding my daypack against my chest. I could hear a dog yapping somewhere then a woman appeared blonde middle-aged thick make-up a bob-cut tight olive-green dress gold necklace earrings all that. Ah she said you're here good good come in is that all you've got meaning my old daypack she laughed when I said yes. Put it there she said put it down come with me I'll show you around. I'm Deidre Fletcher she said but you must call me Mistress did you have a good trip? I nodded and smiled I felt stupid. I put my daypack on the floor where she told me I still didn't know what was going on did the young man say cook?

The first place the Mistress took me was the kitchen a big open kitchen next to the dining room it was like the kitchen at Cook School only better. A big stand-alone eight-burner Supertron hanging rails with S-hooks pots pans skillets woks sieves strainers Wusthof knives four Jon Boos maple chopping boards a Miele blender a Cusipro food mill a hundred other things. Now this is your kitchen the Mistress was saying I think you'll find everything here but if there's anything you need let me know it hasn't been used much but it's yours now I hope you can bring it to life. You will do breakfast and dinner she said breakfast can be simple I will talk to you later about my dinner ideas. You are fully equipped she said if you have any questions now's the time to ask.

She was leaning with her back to the bench her hands spread wide she had a good body serious cleavage she was not bad to look at. Well Mistress I said the only thing I'm not sure about at this stage are the exact terms of my employment. The words came out just like that it felt weird but right. Although I said I expected to move into employment once my training was complete this has come about a bit sooner than I imagined. Please please said the Mistress taking her hands off the bench and holding them out in front of her like a shield I'd prefer you talked your own language here. There was an awkward silence then. You will have a room and a weekly allowance she said don't worry you will be well looked after. I am your cook I said just to make sure. You are our cook she said smiling.

I followed the Mistress out of the kitchen through the dining room into an open living area a huge area dark wood flooring a fireplace plush couches a widescreen TV a coffee table and along one wall big windows and glass doors looking out onto a patio and a big lap pool a shiny barbecue with a hood and past that a deep lush garden and lawn sweeping down a slope into the distance towards a line of old trees. A fluffy little dog was yapping and scratching at the glass. Now this would normally be out of bounds the Mistress was saying you can access the kitchen from the other side I'll show you how to do that later. But first I'll show you your room. We crossed back the way we came my pack was still leaning against the wall I picked it up and followed her across the foyer away from the kitchen up a flight of stairs.

Halfway up we met a girl coming down good-looking straight blonde hair this is Jade said the Mistress Jade this is our new cook but Jade wasn't interested she went on down the stairs. Jade's our baby the Mistress was saying sixteen and a half. Above her is Melody twenty-three I'll introduce you later. Their rooms are on this floor here. We had reached the top of the first set of stairs and the Mistress was pointing down a corridor. Melody Jade she said and down this way she was pointing the other way is our room and Ian's study you will call Ian Master up we go. The next set of stairs was narrow we turned twice left then right next we were standing in a short hallway on the top floor. The ceilings were lower here and the walls and carpet not so clean. There's a spare room down there said the Mistress and a bathroom here she said pushing the door open to see. A small bathroom with a small wind-out window a bath shower basin and toilet. Clean towels on the rack she said. She closed the door again. And this she said opening another door is yours.

The whole time the Mistress was talking and I was thinking over and over what does this mean I couldn't help feeling the pattern was right. There are many paths to the one you want I thought no reason why this shouldn't be one of them. I had learnt a lot at Cook School how to break things down and see them for what they really are a lamb chop for example is not made out the back of a supermarket on a lamb chop machine it is cut from the side of a bleating baby sheep. OK I said now see this.

The Mistress was standing in the middle of a biggish room the ceiling quite low behind her a small window I could see the tops of trees and some sky. First of all it was Ian's billiards room she was saying but when the girls got bigger and Ian got too busy we changed it into a rumpus room but of course they've all got their own TVs and laptops now. She thought about this for a second. We've put some furniture in here for you she said but if there's anything else you need just ask. Against the wall was a single bed with a doona on it girly stickers on the bedhead a chest of drawers on the other wall a portable TV on top and beside that a wardrobe. There was a desk under the window too with a computer and printer a black office chair and in the corner away from the bed a pool table with a sheet over it boxes stacked on top. Make yourself at home said the Mistress we will have a chat about menus later. I'm going out now she said it's just after two I should be back at five. She checked her watch. Well she said backing away towards the door. Lovely to have you here Zac I hope it will work out you can put all that other stuff behind you now everything will be fine. Then she turned and left.

I listened to her footsteps going down the stairs. She'd left her perfume in the room. It was quiet then just a low hum from somewhere birds chirping in the trees I unpacked my bag on the bed there wasn't much and put my clothes in the chest of drawers. In the bottom drawer I found an old note *I am thinking of U* it said. That was funny a light blue piece of paper folded tight the edges worn smooth I pushed it up the back. I put my clock my Larousse my workbook my knives on top of the dresser my truffle in the drawer then lay down on the bed and stared for a while at the ceiling. It was odd after so long sleeping in the bunkhouse with all its windy echoes to be lying like that in a real bed had I died and gone to heaven?

On the wall above me was a big rectangular patch where a flatscreen TV must have been four screw holes and a piece of aerial cable hanging out. The window was half-open but the room still smelled shut up and musty I could hear that low humming noise again the filter pump on the pool. A small white cloud drifted past. There were other sounds too now someone drilling a lawn mower far-off a car going past a school bell in the distance the sound of kids shouting. From somewhere in the house below I could hear muffled female voices the Mistress presumably and someone else. I felt how can I say it very small in that room and at the same time very big.

I lay there for a long time dreaming up what might happen next the patch of blue sky the funny-shaped clouds the sounds of the house and the suburbs like through cotton wool. After a while I must have drifted off then I heard footsteps doors opening and closing music coming on the Mistress calling can you keep it down a little please? A bit after that I heard two voices at the bottom of the stairs then whispering outside my door. I listened for a while but the sounds got quieter I drifted off to sleep again.

When I woke up I was sweating. Someone was knocking and next thing the Mistress is standing inside my room leaning forward saying I'm sorry you must have fallen asleep it's already five o'clock. A proper kind of voice but also a bit naïve even dumb. Would you like to get up now? she said. I said of course and threw my feet onto the floor. I'm sorry I said I was up early this morning working it's a very comfort- able bed I was feeling a bit tired.

All right she said have a wash I'll meet you downstairs. She walked to the window and wound very fast until it was wide open. We need to get some air in here she said but not necessarily to me. I'll get you a fan she said then she was gone and I heard her calling up. Uniforms in the wardrobe! There was a full-length mirror on the inside of the wardrobe door and hanging on the rail three uniforms a white chef's jacket dark trousers black clogs the jackets with my name already embroidered on the pocket. I took off my old clothes put on a uniform went into the bathroom washed my face and combed my hair then came back and checked myself in the big mirror. I've got to say I don't mind saying I cut a pretty fine figure there all that was missing was the toque.

Downstairs the family was waiting the Mistress and her two daughters lined up alongside. They didn't look very enthusiastic. Here he is the Mistress said and she introduced me to them Melody tall and pretty long dark hair not much make-up an honest face Jade skinny long blonde hair milky skin and dark red lipstick. I shook their hands theirs very soft mine with knife and burn scars and a hard callous on the middle finger where the heel of the big knife rubbed. All right then off you go said the Mistress and the daughters went their separate ways Melody gliding very tall and straight but now the Mistress was talking again. All right she said let's pop into the kitchen.

On the bench were two plastic shopping bags which the Mistress started unpacking. A packet lasagne salad greens breakfast cereal a two-litre bottle of orange juice a dozen barn-laid eggs a tube of toothpaste a packet of slimline sanitary pads and a ten-pack of double-A batteries. All the while she was doing this putting the lasagne salad eggs and orange juice into the big Fisher & Paykel fridge the cereal in the cupboards gathering up the other things and holding them to her breast the Mistress was talking. She spoke very fast but I didn't miss a word it didn't matter how or why I ended up here what I needed to know now was what I should be *doing*.

It doesn't matter how hard you try the Mistress was saying it's always difficult keeping a family together they go their separate ways eventually and sure I want my own life back but that doesn't mean I'm going to give up on the idea of a family completely. It's good for us to sit down to a meal together I understand the girls are growing up but while they're still under this roof they're a part of this household aren't they and it wouldn't hurt them to sit down sometimes at the same table and have a civil conversation. I can't think of a night this past three months or more when they haven't eaten takeaway or had an egg on toast. So. You are our live-in cook you have your own room and a weekly allowance to help turn us into a family again. Two meals daily breakfast and dinner breakfast served between seven and ten the evening meal at seven sharp. We will make our own arrangements for lunch. Weekends you will be on call as needed. Daytimes you will shop and prepare and cook and generally keep the kitchen and dining area clean and tidy. I will take you shopping tomorrow. Jade is lactose intolerant you will need to keep this in mind. The pantry is already stocked as you can see the Mistress opened it up you can top it and the fridge up at any time on account. I will cook tonight she said you can rest we will shop together tomorrow.

She had put away the last of the things and was now scrunching up the two plastic bags a bit too hard in her hands. Money doesn't buy everything she was saying it certainly doesn't buy happiness but perhaps it can buy us a little quality time together. My husband she said is a very rich man we are a very rich family we can have whatever we want when we want it but you know I'm going to tell you a secret all I really want is for us to sit down together once a day five days a week as a family and talk. The Mistress opened a cupboard and put the plastic bags in a container attached to the back of the door.

I hadn't said a word my mind was racing a live-in cook an open cheque book a kitchen to die for two daughters a room of my own a TV a computer was someone playing a trick? Are there any questions the Mistress was saying to me and of course there were a million questions like what happened to Cook School? or where is Head Chef? or am I here forever? Instead I asked if I could cook tonight I would be happy to I said. The Mistress smiled the creases around her mouth and eyes very deep. No she said that's all right we will start properly tomorrow.

Next she led me through a door at the other end of the kitchen into a laundry then a drying room then out into the backyard on the other side of the pool. This was the back way. It felt strange being outside again. You will need to go this way from now on she said pointing. We crossed around behind the patio and the pool and entered the house again through a downstairs games area gym equipment a table-tennis table leaning up against the wall a gym ball in the corner then up a separate smaller flight of stairs until we came out onto the second floor near the Mistress's bedroom like before. I took the small stairs to my room. My room. I checked myself in the mirror and straightened the buttons of my jacket.

It was dark outside my stomach was rumbling I hadn't eaten since breakfast back at Cook School when a little while later I heard a knock on the door. It was Jade the youngest she had brought me up a plate. She was wearing pink tracksuit pants and a tight white top her white belly with a silver stud showing. Her hair was clipped up with a comb. Mum said to give you this she said standing in the hall handing it to me. A slab of over-cheesy lasagne and a salad mix with bottled dressing. Thank you I said. And thank you for having me. But Jade wasn't listening she was looking past me into the room her top lip curled up like someone had put something disgusting under her nose. I turned around to see what she was looking at it must have been the bed but when I turned back she was gone. I listened to her footsteps going down the stairs. The meal was not what I was used to but I was so hungry now it didn't matter. After that I sat at the desk for a while listening to the sounds in the house. Yes I thought tomorrow I will shop devise my own menus show these people what I am made of. I took out my workbook and opened the Larousse.

It was strange waking up in my new room the alarm went off just after dawn. All those months in the bunkhouse now here I was the lap of luxury la-de-da. I put on my uniform checked myself in the mirror and went downstairs by the long way to the kitchen. It was funny being in there but good too it was not like I hadn't worked for it. The Master came in already dressed a new suit and tie that's right he said you're here like yesterday was a dream. He took an apple from the bowl on the bench and went out again. I could hear a car outside its motor running then the sound of it driving away.

It was still early about seven but already I could hear Melody up the dog yapping along the edge of the pool. I unloaded the dishwasher from the night before put the dishes away and set the dining room table. There was still no-one around. The breakfast options were pretty limited I would need to go shopping soon but in the meantime there was cereal toast eggs and bacon I made a quick *hollandaise*. Soon the rest of the house was stirring. The Mistress was up I could hear her talking her voice raised then the sound of the front door closing. Shortly after that she poked her head into the kitchen. She was in a mauve silk dressing-gown her hair pinned up her make-up already on. Good morning! she said and she went out again. I made myself a piece of toast and coffee and sat on a stool at the bench.

When Melody came into the kitchen it was like I wasn't there. She was dressed very sharp a knee-length black skirt black boots a bit of red lipstick her hair still wet smelling of herbs and spices. I stood up. Good morning Melody I said what would you like? Listen she said listen to me I don't agree with this I think it's fucked but all right listen she said changing tack I don't want to spoil it for you so poached eggs on toast and a strong cafe latte. She went back into the dining room. I got to work. A saucepan of water on the stove a tablespoon of vinegar in it sourdough bread in the toaster the coffee machine on the coffee ground. The two eggs when they came out were close to perfect I drained them trimmed them laid them on the toast like babies on a bed. I swirled a clover pattern in the top of the coffee and brought everything out to the dining room. Melody was reading the paper her mobile flat on the table she rearranged the paper when I put the things down the salt and pepper grinder just in reach. She waited till I finished she wasn't giving anything away. Will there be anything else? I asked. She shook her head she seemed sad. Is everything all right? I asked. Yes she said everything's fine it looks lovely thanks. I went back to the kitchen.

I heard Melody's mobile beep a couple of times then the sound of it ringing she seemed a busy person too. After a while I heard the scrape of her cutlery go quiet I waited a bit longer then looked back through the doorway into the dining room. She had finished the meal and was playing with her mobile her hair still wet a strand trailing down her shoulder a pointy nose a pretty face and something that made her seem superior I don't know maybe it was just the way she held herself very straight her chin always up a little. I stood at the door for a while then when I thought the moment was right I crept back into the dining room very quiet and stood in the humble spot one step back and off to one side. Is that all? I asked. She didn't look around. Thank you she said. I leaned over and gathered up the dishes. I knew she was going to speak I could almost hear her thoughts shaking themselves ready when I leaned down close to her the sweet herbs and spices coming off her hair very strong in my nostrils but just then Jade appeared in the doorway looking like a long-legged little deer staring at me the stray come in off the street.

She spoke to Melody not to me. Do we have to get him to do our breakfast? she said. She was in short pink striped pyjamas her hair sticking out. Did you hear that thing at seven-thirty she said how are we supposed to sleep with that? All right she said talking to me but not looking at me this is ridiculous but anyway I'll have a bowl of Special K with soy milk am I supposed to sit here? Melody smiled and pulled a chair out for her.

Would you like fruit on your cereal Jade? I asked. Now for the first time Jade really looked at me. What are you doing here? she said. I'm your new live-in cook I said I thought your mother explained it. Jade thought about this for a minute like she was going to take it further but instead she put her head on the table and folded her hands over it. Yes fruit she said but I didn't catch it the first time I had to ask her to repeat it. Yes fruit she said fruit all right fruit.

Back in the kitchen I got the cereal ready and topped it with some canned peaches I found in the pantry that I then quickly caramelised on the stove. Little steps I said little steps. When I brought the bowl back into the dining room Melody was gone and Jade still had her face on the table her arms draped across the back of her head. She looked like she was sleeping. Excuse me I said Jade your cereal is ready. From somewhere I wasn't sure where in the house or outside I heard for the first time the noise she was talking about a drill screeching high to low two or three times in a row. Jade lifted her head and looked at me like it was my fault the drill. Thanks she said put it there. I went back to the kitchen and looked back through the crack in the door at Jade her head half-lifted off the table staring at the bowl of cereal. After a long time she stood up picked up the bowl turned around her pyjama pants all creased at the back and left.

I cleaned up again and started looking through the pantry the cupboards the fridge to make a shopping list. I still had my head in the pantry right up the back among the cans when I heard a voice behind me. It was a tradesman a big guy in his thirties short hair strong face wearing carpenters' overalls. I'm Mark he said you must be the new cook Deidre wants breakfast in the garden. I smoothed down my uniform. Yes I'm the cook I said. Anyway said Mark the tradesman I was coming in to get a cold drink and she asked could you go out and see her she hasn't had breakfast yet. He went to the fridge took a jug of cold cordial from the shelf in the door and poured himself a glass. You'll see a bit of me around here he said I'm working here most days now when I haven't got anything else on. He drank the cordial in one go rinsed his glass put it on the sink and held out his hand. Good to meet you he said shaking my hand and looking at my jacket pocket head down arse up Zac and you'll be right they treat us pretty well around here. He said that last bit with a smile.

I found the Mistress outside in the garden in her dressing-gown sitting at a white-painted wrought-iron table under a tree reading a magazine. The sun was up the sky blue a spring day the weather warm. She'd been waiting for me. Ah she said you're here have you served the girls did they eat and Jadey too? I told her what each of them had the Mistress looked very pleased. *Bon* she said good job now I think it might be my turn did you have anything in mind? I explained how I was working with limited ingredients but I could do a nice eggs benedict if she liked. *Oeufs Benedict* she said oh yes that would be lovely I have that at Massimo's. *Oeufs Benedict* lovely she said.

I found a tablecloth in the dining room brought it back

out and set the table for her. The drilling sound had started up again and now I could see Mark the tradesman a little further on in the garden on a patch of lawn between two big trees building something. A gazebo said the Mistress I'll be having my breakfast in there from tomorrow. The Mistress stared at Mark working for a while imagining I guessed the gazebo finished and herself inside eating *oeufs Benedict* or *sur le plat* or *brouillés au saumon fumé*. I was imagining too. The Master and Mistress taking cocktails at four sitting down to a candlelit dinner soft music playing me in a long white apron serving what would it be a *tranche* of milk veal with a salmon *mousseline* white asparagus spears watercress garnish the two of them placing their cutlery respectfully alongside their plates like they needed time to digest what they had just tasted into every part of their bodies and me now with my own kind of haughtiness standing in the humble position my hands behind my back my chin upraised. Yes who held the power now I thought.

Back in the kitchen I set to work making the best eggs benedict I could under the circumstances whisking a new *hollandaise* getting the water ready adding the vinegar cracking the egg. I threw out three eggs before I was happy but in the end I had two perfect comet-shaped eggs drained and trimmed and arranged on the toast. I wiped off held the plate up to the light tilted it this way and that to check the composition and when I was happy I took it outside. I put it on the table in front of the Mistress bowed a little bow and stepped back.

I could feel the excitement coming off her a quiver of pleasure up her spine she smiled and thanked me then picked up her knife and fork. Mark started hammering down at the gazebo. I bowed again and stepped away. When I went out later to collect the plate I had taken off my uniform I thought that would be a good touch I was in my morning civvies ready to shop but I still did the bow and the did you enjoy your meal? The Mistress said yes very much. Well I said if you don't mind I will get cleaned up now. I took the plate back to the kitchen scraped it and put it in the dishwasher put my uniform in the wash and went back to my room.

So there I was. From nowhere eight months ago to living in one of the fanciest houses working for one of the richest families in town. I thought about Hunna and his little family on their little patch of dirt up in the Valley saying service will never get you anywhere if only he could see me now! Tell them all when you see them all those other losers where I am now ask if they're happy with their miserable little lives. The Master was on the rich list last year at number eighty-two I looked it up on the computer make sure you tell them that too.

When I came downstairs later that morning to start our shopping trip the Mistress was out the front dark pants high heels and a bright blue top trying to sort out the cars. In the garage the Master's silver BMW beside it the Mistress's dark blue Mercedes and behind them in the driveway Melody's dark green Subaru and Jade's pink Prius with the L plates in the windows. The Mistress couldn't get the Mercedes out. Melody drove her car out into the street past the front hedge and back into the driveway again from the other side then she did the same with the Prius. The Mistress backed the Mercedes out and drove it up to where I was waiting on the steps. Jump in jump in she said like it was me who was holding things up. We drove away the tyres crunching on the gravel and behind us I could see Melody moving her car up again. There was a tangle of different coloured shopping bags in the back. The Mistress took a blue freezer brick out of her handbag and gave it to me. Put that in the blue one she said. And this is for you she said and she handed me a mobile. Jade's got a new one there's still eighteen months left on the plan. I put the mobile in my pocket and the blue brick in the bag.

All right the Mistress was saying as we drove down the tree-lined street first we'll go to Ray's for the meat then

Organicasa for the fruit and veg I'll introduce you to Martin and Meredith there's a pad and pen in the glovebox let's write a few things down. I found a Biro and a little black notebook then I felt the car slow down. The Mistress had pulled over to the side of another tree-lined street the same as the one we'd just left. She had her hands hard on the wheel and was staring straight ahead her chin was bobbing up and down it took me a long time to realise she was crying. I didn't know what to do. She sucked in her lips and held one hand flat a little wall in front of her mouth until she had composed herself. She moved two fingers under her eyes barely touching the skin trying to get rid of the tears without messing up the makeup. I'm all right I'm all right she was saying as if I'd asked. I usually do this on my own she said dear me. She did that thing with the two fingers again wiping under her eyes until it looked like she'd recovered then she said all right again like again it was an answer to something I said. Then she put the car in gear and we drove.

I thought we might have some red meat said the Mistress. It was like the crying thing never happened. I nodded and said whatever she preferred. We were driving through the same quiet streets with big trees arching over the road high hedges fences gates long driveways and glimpses of big houses. Yes I thought even though their houses are bigger and better it was like they were ashamed to show them they kept them right up the back. I wouldn't be embarrassed I thought there'd be no high hedge in front of my place I'd want the peasants to see. If we could the Mistress was saying I'd like to alternate as much as possible over the seven days say two nights red meat two nights white meat two nights seafood one night vegetarian but of course the recipes themselves are up to you and of course we can be flexible. Cooking's not a science it's an art isn't it? She turned to me and smiled like I should be impressed it was the first hint she'd given that I might be a cook who had opinions so I thought now was a good time to answer. Yes I said but that doesn't mean it should be self-indulgent. There was a nice silence after that. Head Chef at Cook School I said carefully told us we need to subjugate ourselves to become strong that means I said we should never forget that our purpose is to serve that's what gives what we do meaning. The Mistress went quiet then I don't know if it was because I mentioned service like that or Head Chef I couldn't be sure. I decided to be careful and keep my mouth shut silence is service too.

After a short while we came out onto a main street there was a dip in the road a train crossing at the bottom and a station alongside it. There were big trees here too arching across the tables on the footpath in front of a café a row of shops on either side about a dozen in all. The Mistress drove slowly past the shops a drycleaner's a florist's a butcher's a gift shop a chemist a baker's a greengrocer's with table displays out the front then she turned into a side street with a blue parking sign. There was a small customer carpark around the back with about twenty spaces marked out in white about half-a-dozen cars similar to ours. We walked back to the main street through a narrow arcade past a small gourmet sandwich bar a beauty therapist's a jeweller's and came out next to the gift shop. A woman was coming out carrying a little gift-wrapped parcel the Mistress must have known her next thing she was putting a hand on my back and pushing me forward. I was carrying the two empty shopping bags one green one blue the blue one with the freezer brick in it. This is my friend Libby said the Mistress Libby this is Zac my new cook. She said it like it was a natural thing but at the same time something special. We're just off to do some shopping said the Mistress. Come round for dinner I'll call you she said and she led me to the butcher's.

It was a quaint little shopping strip all restored old-fashioned benches and streetlamps rubbish bins in wood-panelled boxes the butcher's even had a bell that went ping when you entered. This is Ray the Mistress was saying a big man in a butcher's apron was walking towards us from behind the counter wiping his hands on a cloth. Deidre! he said look at you you Hollywood starlet with your little boy you've done something with your hair. The Mistress put a hand underneath her hair like she was checking it in a mirror. Ray this is Zac the new cook I was telling you about he started today he's going to be doing the shopping from now on so I want you to do the right thing. Ray laughed he was a meaty-looking man grey and balding a bit saggy around the eyes and a bit fat around the middle he held out a hand for me a chunky hard-working hand with half a finger missing. Nice to meet you Zac he said don't worry I'll look after you only the best cuts for Deidre as always eh Deidre now what would you like today?

And that's when it struck me I had been a servant that morning in my new house maybe even a cook but had I been a chef? Because what is a chef if he doesn't source and control every element of the plate right up to the final garnish? A chef is a slave but he is also a creator he should be completely in charge. What do you want? asked Ray the butcher it's not many times I've been asked that what do you think you're doing more likely.

I tried not to take too long answering the Mistress had already turned towards me like the question was for me. I'd like a nice cut of lamb I said the best you've got a backstrap maybe to do into *rondelles* or some loin for *noisettes* something from the *côtes premières* nice and tender not too much fat. And some bones for stock I said veal shanks and knuckles I'm going to do a red wine and rosemary *jus*. The Mistress was smiling Ray the butcher had a blank sort of look but then after I finished his eyes lit up all sparkly blue he threw back his head and laughed. Well well he said to the Mistress you've got yourself a real one here! Sure buddy he said to me still laughing like I was an old friend. I wasn't yet but I would be. Make a friend of your supplier Fabian said.

The doorbell rang and another woman came in. The Mistress knew her too. They started chatting loudly then softer in a whisper their heads to one side gossiping then the new woman nodded like they should go outside. The bell tinkled again and the two women stood on the footpath in front of the display window the meat trays glistening gossiping mouth to ear. Come out the back said Ray.

It was cool out there I could hear the air-conditioner humming a big ancient wooden chopping block in the middle of the room with a side of beef on it and behind that overhead a stainless steel rail with more carcasses hanging from the hooks. Ray slid open the big coolroom door and came back out with a lamb carcass draped over his shoulder about twenty kilo good quality from what I could see. He hung the beef carcass up on a hook dumped the lamb on the block and started sharpening his knife.

So you're the cook up at the Fletchers' he said where did you train? I did eight months at culinary college I said hands-on intense we lived on a farm learned everything paddock to plate. Ray let out a low whistle but he didn't say anything. I didn't finish the course though I said I was hand-picked to come here. Ever heard of Mandalong lamb? he said. I said I had read about it. Well sonny this is one said Ray and he patted the carcass on the rump. Grain-fed tenderstretched three weeks' aged this is the best lamb in the country and this here he said he was pointing at the loin is the best cut of lamb anywhere in the world. He nodded towards it like I should touch. Breeders butchers chefs they all judge by touch I pushed a finger then a thumb into the flesh. And you're going to cook for them every night? said Ray sharpening his knife again. Every breakfast and dinner I said. And will you be fucking the daughters? He didn't look up but I could feel his smile. Not both at once I said.

That gave Ray the biggest laugh I reckon he'd ever had he slapped the carcass with both hands flat and threw back his head. Cook my arse! he said. I'm not sure what he meant by that I didn't want to ask but then we both heard the doorbell ring again and the Mistress shouting *heelloo!* When I came back out into the shop she was looking at her watch. Come on she said quickly we need to get to Organicasa before they close for lunch. Ray smiled and said come back later he'd have a nice cut ready. He held up his butchering knife and gave me a wink. Trust me I'm a butcher he said. Even the Mistress smiled at that.

Next the Mistress led me to Organicasa a few doors down and introduced me to the owners Martin and Meredith new hippies in their thirties both with their hair pulled back both with healthy-looking skin. Meredith had a floral dress Martin a pink shirt they looked very stressed for organic greengrocers they were holding one end each of a display table trying to move it inside. Marty Merry said the Mistress this is the new cook I was telling you about I hope we're not too late. They smiled gritting their teeth and dragged the table inside. They close the shop at lunch whispered the Mistress to take a lunchbox to their daughter at school. She seemed very impressed with this. I hope it's all right she said loudly to Martin and Meredith we just need to grab a few things. Martin and Meredith had got the table in now and Martin was walking back out towards us. I'm just going over to the chemist said the Mistress and I watched her quick-stepping across the street.

Hello said Martin smiling what can we do for you? I told him I was doing lamb with a rosemary and red wine *jus* I needed whatever was fresh asparagus for entrée maybe then for mains a side of vegetables whatever looks good brown onions for my stock shallots garlic and rosemary for my *jus*. While I was talking I was looking around at the display stands all made out of raw timber each variety with its own separate compartment the potatoes for example six different varieties each in its little box or beans three varieties half-a-dozen different kinds of apples. All right said Martin let's have a look.

He led me first to the root vegetable display Dutch carrots baby red carrots baby white carrots baby white turnips baby leeks all glistening fresh. He took a little Dutch carrot from its compartment and held it up. It was a beautiful-looking thing squat and slender brilliant orange with little droplets of water still clinging to it. Martin held one end of this carrot between his finger and thumb and snapped it in half very theatrically with the finger and thumb of his other hand. You could actually hear it snap. He took a bite from his half and gave the other to me. This was as good as any carrot I pulled from the loamy earth just after dawn in the garden at Cook School crunchy tender fresh.

I'll take half a kilo of mixed I said. Martin weighed a handful of baby vegetables and put them in a brown paper bag with an Organicasa logo on the side then wrote something down in his pad. We went around the shop picking bits and pieces here and there brown onions loose asparagus spears watercress a handful of nasturtium flowers two bunches of rosemary one with a good topping of pink blooms. I had five brown paper bags in all I put what I could in the green shopping bag and carried the rest. I was saving the blue bag for the meat.

Meredith joined us out the front she had her hair down now and was holding a clear plastic lunchbox with little compartments inside I could see chopped carrot celery cheese some strawberries and the name Verity written in texta on the top. I thought you were going to be European she said. The Mistress came hurrying back across the street. Thank you Marty thank you Merry she said here's the number like I said text him early come on come on she said to me and she led me away again. Behind us I could hear the shutter of Organicasa coming down Martin and Meredith putting on their helmets and getting on their bikes. Meredith's had a grey plastic kid's seat on the back.

Next we went to a shop called Precious Fine Foods a big display window cans jars and bottles of just about everything an antique door the paint roughly stripped and Precious Fine Foods written over the top of the window in sloping gold letters. A supermarket but a fancy one. If you wanted a litre of milk say there were three different kinds all organic even one in an old-fashioned glass bottle. For the eggs there was a special wooden display table with egg-holes in it all different shapes and sizes whites and browns bits of feathers and bird shit on them. There were fourteen varieties of olive oil and not one I'd seen before and in the fridge cabinet a dozen cheeses all small and special fresh olives in tubs eight different kinds even a pat of butter on a board.

The owner was Sanjif an Indian guy late-twenties good-looking well-dressed he came out from behind the counter nodding almost bowing saying Miss Deidre Miss Deidre. The Mistress introduced me to him. Ah he said he had a toothy smile you are the cook and when he shook my hand he turned it side-on like he was showing me who was boss. A cook is a very good idea he said to the Mistress we should all have a cook! He took me shelf by shelf around the shop olive oils vegetable oils sunflower oils sesame oils macadamia oils almond oils truffle oils condiments spreads organic flour stoneground flour buck-wheat flour rice flour soy flour corn flour white sugar caster sugar raw sugar brown sugar Demerara sugar palm sugar table salt rock salt sea salt lake salt imported and fresh handmade pastas jars of capers olives artichoke hearts marinated fetta on one shelf even a jar of black truffles bottles of wine local and imported nothing under fifty dollars some two hundred or more.

When we got back to the counter Sanjif went behind it and cut me a little corner of cheese from the cabinet with a small bone-handled knife. *Pont-l'Évêque* he said from Gippsland a little dairy husband and wife we just got it in this morning Miss Deidre please. It was very good all right very gooey inside a salty rind you could smell the cow shed in there seventy-two dollars a kilo. Sanjif gave us each a small white napkin and a very tiny plastic cup like the ones Dad used to have his tablets in with filtered water in it. Sanjif waited till we'd wiped our fingers and drank our little cups then he took our rubbish from us and put it in the bin behind the counter.

All right he said now Chef what can I do for you today? I liked that he called me Chef. I ordered some Regaleali extra virgin olive oil the bottle very slim and elegant Tartuflanghe truffle oil a jar each of goose and duck fat a packet of Bolivian rose salt Malabar black peppercorns two dozen organic free-range eggs a block of Belgian dark chocolate half a kilo of artisan butter a bottle of fresh farm milk and half-a-dozen mixed bottles of wine. Sanjif put the butter and milk in a special little chiller bag the other stuff in sturdy brown paper bags with string handles and Precious Fine Foods written in sloping writing on the side. He came out from behind the counter to give it all to me. From a backstreet slum somewhere I thought and now here he was a small businessman in the land of milk and honey. Watch I said. And learn. Sanjif smiled and bowed.

Last the Mistress led me to the café with tables outside under a big spreading tree. The name of the café was Serendipity. Me and the Mistress had barely turned up the Mistress picking a table me standing around with the bags when a young waitress in a spotless white apron with a short black apron over that her hair clipped up an order pad in one hand a black pen in the other came out of the café and guided us by pointing with the pen to an empty table under the tree. Good afternoon said the waitress to both of us but to me with a little wince.

The Mistress said we would be having lunch that was a surprise and asked the waitress could she bring two menus please? She told me to put down my bags and pulled a chair up for herself. This was going to be awkward I could feel it. The waitress went away. Should I get the meat now I asked I couldn't think of anything else to say but the Mistress said no we'll pick it up later that's all right. I pulled up a chair and sat down. The waitress came back with two menus. She told us about the specials board in particular a steak of pan-seared line-caught tuna on a bed of wild rocket and candied walnuts with smoked tomatoes and zucchini flowers. The Mistress ordered the tuna and a glass of Cloudy Bay sauvignon blanc I ordered the quail *terrine* with *foie gras* orange segments and pistachios and a glass of water. The waitress wrote everything down and went away again.

Twenty-four hours in the house most of that time spent with the Mistress but it only just struck me then with a big awkward silence between us where I had actually ended up I mean out shopping with this rich woman sitting down to lunch in a classy café ordering quail *terrine*. Take a photo I thought and send it to the social workers or that crew-cut cop with the sneer.

There was no-one else at the café except an old couple at a table inside and a young guy in a suit with a cup of coffee at the outside table furthest from us talking on his phone. The waitress brought the Mistress's wine and for me a glass of water. Well Zac the Mistress said once the waitress was gone I think it's time you told me something about yourself if you're going to be living in our house I suppose we should get to know you. It was a surprise all right that she said that but it was odd too very odd because she wasn't looking me in the eye but at a spot somewhere on my forehead.

I suppose you've got family she said you do have family I hope? She was moving a salt grinder sideways. I've got one sister I said her name is Tash and a mum who lives on her own. And your father? asked the Mistress. He died about a month ago while I was still at Cook School I said but I was too busy to go home. The waitress came back with our meals and put a plate each in front of us. The Mistress took up her cutlery. And you want to be a chef? she said like that was the thing we had been talking about all along. Yes I said I want to be a chef but the journey will be a long one I have only just begun. I told her about my eight months at Cook School what I'd cooked what I'd learnt. My background might be lowly I said but I had set very high standards for myself. I had not come this far I assured the Mistress all the while eating my quail *terrine* to plate up run-of-the-mill tried and true no-star restaurant meals. Like the great Carême at ten thrown out on the streets given a job in a low-class restaurant apprenticed to one of the best pastry chefs in Paris and who ended his days working for Baron de Rothschild I want to serve those above me and never fail to surprise. Why shouldn't we enjoy the good life I said pointing to the Mistress's wine and the piece of tuna speared on the end of her fork we've worked hard for it haven't we? We dwell I said in a land of sunshine and fertile soils why shouldn't we enjoy its fruits? I sipped my water. It tasted like that melted snow I brought back in a jar that time coming down the mountain in the back seat with Tash and her girlfriend she had big bosoms too just like the Mistress I remember. This was a convict colony I said rum and buggery with a history like that you've got to try hard and then even harder again if you want to get as sophisticated as the French. It's not going to come naturally.

The Mistress laid her knife and fork on her plate. And your ambition? she said interpreting everything I said I suppose as being somehow tied up with this. Would you like perhaps one day to run your own restaurant? Yes I said I would very much like to one day run my own restaurant and I was sure I would but little steps I said and then great strides I would not get ahead of myself. The Mistress moved her knife and fork so they were lying parallel to each other. And what will be the name of your restaurant? she said. I told her Insouciance and explained what it meant and how I found it in the dictionary when I was looking up insolvent. It means you have no worries I said and that's how I want my customers to feel. In my restaurant the customer won't need to think for example just when they're wondering what to order my Head Waiter will be there leaning over quietly pointing out something to them and that something will always be just right. Same with my Sommelier. In Insouciance we'll sort everything for you all your wants and needs people will come to my restaurant from every corner of the earth not just for the food which of course will be sensational but because we will read all their wants know all their needs give them what they didn't even know they needed all they have to do is relax.

I sure had babbled on all right but I hadn't lost the Mistress yet she was listening to my every word. I had been talking so much I hadn't finished my meal she waited while I put my knife and fork on the plate parallel like hers. I felt overheated I must have been blushing I could feel the damp sweat under my arms but I felt good it was a long time since I'd talked.

I wanted to say more about how Insouciance was in the future and in the meantime of course all my service was for her and her family but now the waitress was back asking did we enjoy our meals. Well. Here was a chance I thought I couldn't let it go. Actually no I said the meal was unsatisfactory. The Mistress looked up. The quail was inferior quality I said cage-bred and overfed the *terrine* what's more was overcooked. As for the oranges well they were not only not sweet but slightly sour. Thank you I said pushing the plate towards her. She picked it up. I looked at the Mistress her face stony she either thought I was a wanker or a genius. The waitress kept her cool and took the plate away the Mistress took a small make-up mirror from her purse and checked her face. When the waitress came back with the bill the Mistress put her credit card on top and I could see where my meal had been crossed out. Well said the Mistress a bit too loudly like she had been thinking about something else we'd better get our meat from Ray's and get this shopping home!

Ray was out the back with the bandsaw going I had to yell a couple of times to get him to hear. He came out and saw me then went back and came out again with my packages. He opened the first one up on the counter. There were two lamb loin backstraps cut perfect glistening almost alive a slight smear of creamy fat. Ray could see me looking he knew I approved he wrapped them up again took a notebook from behind the counter wrote a few figures in it with the pen he kept behind his ear then he pushed my two packages across the counter the other one the bones. All right he said let me know how you go there's my number there ring me early and I'll tell you what's good I'm here at six-thirty sharp. There was a black and gold sticker sealing the packages with Ray's Fine Meats and an address and phone number on it. Can you get me a pheasant? I said. I wrote my new mobile number down and put it on the counter. Ray threw back his head and laughed. Son I can get you an elephant if you want!

Carrying all the shopping the fridge bag in one hand the green bag in the other I followed the Mistress back to her car. She opened the boot I put the things in then joined her in the front. I'm sure you will fulfil your dreams she said but straight ahead like she was talking to the windscreen. That was it she didn't say anything else.

When we got back to the house it was already mid-afternoon my stock still wasn't on I had a hundred things to do. The Mistress was shouting up at Melody's window to get her to come down and move the cars I told her I would need to get started on my preparation it was already late and might I please be excused? The Mistress was a bit surprised by that but impressed too if anyone ever cooked in this house I'm sure they never started at three in the afternoon. I left her in the driveway took the shopping inside went upstairs put on new whites came back down and closed the kitchen door. In short order I got my stock bones baking caramelised some onions added them to the tray then found a big pot that would hold about five litres. While the bones and onions were browning I unpacked all the shopping and sorted my ingredients into courses entrée my asparagus mains my lamb backstraps baby vegetables watercress and nasturtium flowers milk eggs and chocolate for dessert.

It was good being in my own kitchen a real kitchen with everything I needed I was master of my domain. Sure I was still learning my way around but that was part of the fun already I'd rearranged the shelves in the fridge cleared a top drawer next to the stove for the bits and pieces I would use most organised the stuff hanging above it and brought the bedside lamp down from my room to set up on the bit of bench closest to the dining room door for my pass. A chef needs to stamp his personality on his kitchen if you're coming into my kitchen to work you need to do things my way put things back where you got them stir your sauce in the direction I say.

Time went by quietly then in my kitchen all the awkwardness I felt out shopping with the Mistress had faded. I felt good in my skin in my uniform my name on the pocket with all my things just where I wanted. I heard the occasional noise outside or in the house at one point the clickety-clack of the Mistress's heels on the parquetry floor stopping at the kitchen door to listen. *Yes he's in there busy* then clickety-clack away again. Later there was the sound of the front door slamming and voices in the living room. It must have been Jade home from school.

After I'd got my stock simmering and had all my pans and utensils laid out I went by the outside way to my room where I sat for a while at my desk typing up that night's menu. The printer was an old bubblejet way too loud in the quiet of that room I made five copies in all four for the family and one for myself that I would date and file in the drawer so I could keep track of what I'd done. For entrée warm asparagus spears with Regaleali extra virgin olive oil and cracked Malabar black pepper for mains grain-fed Mandalong lamb loin *rondelles* with a rosemary and red wine *jus* served with a *mesclun* of fresh baby vegetables garnished with nasturtium flowers and for dessert a simple baked chocolate custard finished with a dusting of icing sugar and a rosemary flower garnish.

When the printer went quiet I heard noises coming to me through the open window it was Melody and her boyfriend Nick arguing. They had the patio doors open she was yelling at him he was laughing a forced raucous laugh I could hear the Mistress's voice too trying to calm them down. I wasn't sure what they were arguing about but I guessed it must be me. I knew not everyone was happy having me here but I couldn't worry about that you win over your customers by impressing them with your talent not stressing about what they think. They will come around.

After a while the argument quietened down it was just Nick and the Mistress now the Mistress trying to keep the peace then after that down below in the games room beside the pool I could hear the sound of the exercise bike getting furiously pedalled. Pretty soon that noise stopped too and then it was just silence then the sound of some music coming from Jade's room on the floor below. It was five-thirty. I put my things away turned off the computer and gathered up my menus. Melody was in the pool I could hear the gentle splashing the nice even strokes up and down up and down then at each end the slight pause and the turn. I stood at the window out of the light and watched her for a while.

At five-forty-five I was back in the kitchen prepping

for a seven o'clock service four covers in all I was already in the zone. Fabian talked about the zone. My stock had been simmering for a while it could have done with longer but a quick taste told me it was good. A good deep flavour I learned this from Fabian don't put celery and carrot in your pot that only diminishes the flavour of the meat. I ladled some of this liquid into a small saucepan for reduction closer to the time. At six-forty I set the dining room table and put a menu down at each place. At six-fifty I checked the set of my custards and got the water on for my asparagus. The Mistress came through all high and hyper yes yes good good she said she took a bottle of pinot noir from the door of the fridge and a glass from one of the cupboards and went out again. I carefully tied the asparagus tips into four little bunches and dipped them in the water.

Here's what happened. Seven o'clock my asparagus blanched and drying I opened the door a crack. I could see the Mistress sitting in there all uptight looking around anxiously. Down the far end of the table was Jade done up with eyeliner and lipstick in a black mini-skirt. The other seats were empty. Patience they say in that first half-hour stay calm have it all laid out and ready to go when it comes it will come in a rush. I was anxious though I wanted my asparagus tips warm not cold but to reheat them would spoil them I put them closer to the stove. I decanted some olive oil into a little jug and put that near the stove too. I double-checked everything. Every tick of the clock now meant I would need to work faster and fault-lessly later on.

Then bang seven past seven the Mistress comes in through the door from the dining room and says all right let's go. She was wearing a red evening dress with high heels and lots of jewellery. I plated up the asparagus a nice higgledy-piggledy pile a thin spiral of glistening yellow-green olive oil fading out to drips and last a quick snap of the pepper grinder so the black specks tumbled off the asparagus hill out onto the white field of the plate. I adjusted a few asparagus spears and with a plate in each hand backed my way into the dining room.

My guests were seated and waiting but not the guests I expected. The Master wasn't there and in his place Nick was picking the label off a bottle of Stella Artois. Melody was beside him her back very straight her eyes fixed on the table. I stood behind the Mistress for a few seconds wondering what to do but she was already turning and talking to me. Put them down put them down she was saying and go and get the others the Master has been held up but Nick is here we're all here together and this looks lovely well! I told her it was warm fresh asparagus spears with extra virgin olive oil and cracked pepper. Ooh she said. I put a plate each down in front of her and Jade and went back to get the others. When I came back the Mistress was excited almost glowing I could see a smile in the corner of Nick's mouth a steely gaze from Melody a screwed-up face already from Jade I guess she didn't want to smudge her lipstick. I put the rest of the plates down and withdrew.

When I got back to the kitchen the Creuset grill was smoking. My two lamb backstraps I had already massaged with a little oil and rested at room temperature now in a small saucepan I sautéed off my garlic and shallots added red wine chopped rosemary and a ladle of stock and got my *jus* reducing. I put the backstraps on the grill and cooked them fast smoking and flaring until the surface was sealed and intersected by eight to ten uniform diagonal black charcoal lines the whole thing a minute each side then onto a warm dish covered and rested on the bottom rack of the open oven. I went back in to collect the entrée plates Jade had eaten nothing Nick was on his second Stella he must have had his own stash somewhere the others had finished theirs and were quiet. I said I hoped everyone enjoyed their entrées but I didn't wait for an answer and whisked the plates away.

Back in the kitchen I dropped the trimmed vegetables into boiling water stirred and checked my *jus* and prepared the lamb for carving. My backstraps would be cut into twenty mil *rondelles* arranged three a plate at ten o'clock in a scallop design at two o'clock my vegetables and tying the plate together from the *rondelles* at ten through nine to just past six o'clock a splash a smear then a drip-line of *jus* the lamb topped only on the central *rondelle* with two or three shoots of chilled crisp watercress.

My lamb was perfect I don't mind saying browned and slightly crusty on the outside on the inside a magnificent candy red fading through pink to pale pink to brown. I carved the lamb set my four warmed plates on the pass and arranged my *rondelles*. I drained the vegetables tossed them lightly in olive oil arranged them rough-and-ready-style and garnished them with nasturtium flowers then strained and boiled off my *jus* stirring and checking and sticking my finger in until it was just right. With a mini-ladle in one hand and my small saucepan in the other I bent over very low and very close at the pass and gave my *rondelles* a splash a smear then a dribble. Last a little watercress garnish held delicately between thumb and forefinger and dropped so it falls like a leaf from a tree. My four plates were done.

But this time back in the dining room the atmosphere had changed. Melody was gone Nick was finishing his third beer the other two empty with their labels picked off. He was starting to get pissed. The Mistress too now on her third glass of pinot her cheeks flushed her eyes slightly glazed. Ah she said when I came in look at this everyone look at this look what he's done! I put the plates down one by one all except the one that would have been Melody's.

They looked good all right the big white plates against the white tablecloth the browns and pinks and greens and yellows the spring freshness of the flowers a work of art I don't mind saying. When I put his plate down in front of him Nick leaned back a long way his arms out wide the stubby of beer dangling between his fingers a big theatrical expression of surprise.

The Mistress was giving him the stare. Jade had her earbuds in slumped in the chair all grumpy and slutty the strap of her cotton top falling off one shoulder. I stepped back into the humble position and waited still holding Melody's plate up close to my chest.

This is excellent said Nick his arms still spread trying to get my eye look at this Deidre this is classy stuff all right what is it? I rattled it off. Grain-fed Mandalong lamb loin *rondelles* with a rosemary and red wine *jus* and a watercress garnish served with fresh root vegetables finished with Regaleali extra virgin olive oil and a nasturtium flower garnish. And you learned this at school? he said. It's my own dish I said based on a classic recipe but the main thing is the quality of the lamb I have spent some time learning about lamb I hope this is evident in the dish. It certainly looks good doesn't it Deidre said Nick it's a pity Melody didn't want to join us how long were you at Cook School? He'd had a few beers we all get funny when we've had a few beers. Eight months I told him it might have been longer but then I was given this job. And were you happy with your training? said Nick. Please Nick said the Mistress it's getting cold. But it was like Nick hadn't heard. It didn't quite work out did it he said but you've got on with your life all the same you've made something of yourself doesn't matter where you come from you've taken your opportunities I mean Deidre how magnificent is this?

The Mistress had given up she was staring at her meal

the knife and fork still lying beside the plate her glass of pinot in front of her lips. I would need to listen to Nick that was all right a chef always listens no matter how annoying the customer it's by listening to every petty little thing that you get the power over them. Look bow listen.

You know Melody thinks this is all wrong said Nick you being our house slave I'm afraid we've been having some arguments about it. I tell her you're here by choice that slavery's been abolished I mean this is Australia for chrissakes it's the twenty-first century isn't it? It's a free country and if you want to be Deidre and Ian's house boy well that's your choice I mean who are we to stop you? Melody likes to get on her high horse she thinks we've got a social justice issue here but it's not a social justice issue it's a freedom of choice issue the chance to move up and follow your dream. No-one needs to do anything they don't want to anymore.

Now said Nick correct me if I'm wrong but I reckon you probably come from a crap-poor family from the wrong side of the tracks you can see it in you even while you're bowing all that jealousy and resentment but listen Chef let's be honest where would you rather be in your little outer suburban crap-hole or in a mansion like this in one of the best streets in Melbourne? That's what Melody doesn't understand she got infected at uni doing soft-cock arts subjects but you and I know the real world's got nothing to do with nanny-state socialism looking after those worse off than us by giving them just enough to make them happy and keep them where they are. Fuck that I say excuse me Deidre fuck that I say every man for himself. If you want to climb to the top by starting here cooking for us practising your dishes getting better every time I'm sorry Deidre he said turning to her but what the fuck is wrong with that laissez-faire capitalism's not dead yet and this guy's entitled to his share of the proceeds just like every-one else.

Nick was looking at the Mistress but the Mistress wasn't looking at him she was staring over her wine glass at the lamb getting cold on her plate. The silence was broken by the sound of a knife and fork clinking. It was Jade still with her earbuds in completely oblivious the tinny treble sound of treacle pop bleeding out into the room. She cut a piece of lamb swirled it around in the *jus* and put it in her mouth. Mmm she said this is yummy to no-one in particular. The Mistress put down her wine glass and picked up her knife and fork. Mmm she said chewing. Nick emptied his stubby of beer and pushed it to the centre of the table. You've got to talk to Melody Deidre he said if you want your own cook what's wrong with that she's breaking my balls over this. Please Nick said the Mistress before putting another forkful in her mouth. Nick picked up his knife and fork too.

Excuse me I said I wanted to have the last word if you don't mind me saying this lamb dish would be best enjoyed with a glass of pinot noir would you like me to put your beers in the fridge? That got Nick wrong-footed just right even the Mistress smiled at that. I'll bring you a glass I said and I leaned down under his side of the table and picked up the leftover six-pack. Please tell Melody I said standing back that I appreciate her concern but that I am happy with my position here and the best way for me to show her this would be to let me cook for her.

I turned and went back to the kitchen put the beers in the fridge and the leftover plate of food on the bench then gave it a moment and returned with a wine glass for Nick and a second bottle of pinot. Everything was quiet now except for the clink of knives and forks and the tinny music from Jade's earbuds. I poured a glass of pinot for Nick turning and lifting the bottle professionally at the end then with the tips of two fingers only on the base of the stem I slid the glass across the table in front of him and quietly put the new bottle down.

There was a lesson I thought don't get tongue-tied let your cooking speak that's the best weapon you have. It was all quiet in the dining room then I cleaned up the kitchen got the first load of dishes in checked the set of my custards and took them out of the fridge. After a while I could hear the Mistress's voice they must have finished the mains so I went in to collect the plates. Nick was gone his meal half-eaten his wine half-drunk. Jade had finished hers and was sitting with one leg up over the arm of the chair thumbing her mobile phone. The Mistress was talking loudly on her phone to a friend. Lamb she was saying exquisitely done you've never tasted anything like it Libby and the sauce on top it was made in heaven you really *must* come over ah she said suddenly seeing me here he is now I'm talking to Libby she said I told her she must come over so you can cook for us both.

I smiled and bowed she was sozzled all right but I didn't mind so long as she ate and smiled. Of course I said. Now please she was saying as I picked up her plate Libby's asking what you did with the meat? I explained how it was fast-grilled then rested warm in an open oven the *jus* I made from my own stock. Magnificent! she said both to me and the phone. It was absolutely magnificent Lib Jadey did you enjoy your meal? Jade didn't hear she had her earbuds in. I picked up the plates Jade's last she still had her leg over the chair I could see her red knickers showing.

The Mistress was still talking on the phone I waited for a pause before I asked would she like dessert? Yes lovely she said and another glass of wine thank you I don't know what happened to Nick but don't worry about him he's a lovely boy really just half a glass thank you that'll do. I put the bottle back on the table and the Mistress went back to her conversation. With my spare hand I went to pick up Nick's wine glass but when I did Jade slid her hand across and grabbed it. She gave me a look it wasn't hard to read. Leave it there it's mine it said or I'll tell Mum you were looking up my skirt. I took away my hand and let Jade slide the wine glass to her side of the table. With the dirty plates lined up along one arm I bowed to them all and withdrew.

Last thing in the kitchen was to dust my chocolate custards and place a little pink rosemary flower on top. Back in the dining room I put the two chocolate custards down. I'm going to eat it in my room Mum said Jade but the Mistress didn't hear. She was already holding her spoon. Jade picked up her custard and left. Now what's this the Mistress was saying still staring with her spoon in midair at the little bowl on the table in front of her I hope I can fit it in. She laughed at that and looked up to see who was listening but it was only me there. French-style baked chocolate egg custard with a rosemary flower garnish I said. The Mistress looked approvingly at me her eyes wobbling nearly as much as her head. Can I just say she said before we finish that it has been a most extraordinary meal I'm sure we will be very pleased with you thank you very good. It took me a few seconds to realise she'd finished with me. I bowed and retreated to the kitchen. Yes. I had sourced prepped cooked and served everything myself from start to finish. I had been like Fabian said cool under fire I did not get rattled I had cut my coat to fit my cloth but I did not compromise once on any element of any dish. And every dish a success. I had done good. Next time I would do better.

I spent a while cleaning up. I put Melody's leftovers in the fridge and made up a small plate for myself with the backstrap ends and asparagus bits warmed it in the microwave and ate it standing at the bench. The flair had gone out of it all right but I could still taste how good it had been. When I went back in to the dining room the Mistress was gone. She had taken her glass with her I could hear her talking in the living room I picked up the dessert dishes cleaned the table and wiped it down. Last of all I poured myself a glass just one there was no harm in that. I went to the laundry took off my whites and put them in the machine then glass in hand I watched through the little round window the clothes going round and round.

That was nice the afterglow thinking about what I did wrong and how I would correct it next time my cheeks flushed my t-shirt wet the burn on my left hand where I splashed it with oil still throbbing the wine dissolving in my veins filling them with warmth. I was a chef all right I was on my way up. I remembered the look on Head Chef's face when he laid open his palms that day to show us the dish lying on the bench something distant almost psychotic pulsing behind his eyes the stillness after the frenzy like one of those crazy painters or the conductor after the big climax just before the applause. A look of triumph and surprise. That's how I felt staring at my chef's whites tumbling around in the machine a guy who twelve months ago couldn't boil an egg.

A bit after that I heard noises. They must have had the big French doors open to the patio they were arguing again. I heard doors slamming then the Mistress's voice then Melody yelling out the front a car starting up and revving then dying down a door slamming more yelling a different car starting up a crunch of gears then a whine as it reversed then another car getting moved then another the sound of the first revving again its tyres spinning on the gravel then turning into the street and driving away. It was quiet then I heard Melody yell no Mum it's not right then a door slam then silence. When the cycle finished I took the clothes out and put them in the dryer. I would need to spend some time on tomorrow's menu and check my inventories before bed. No rest for the wicked like Dad always said.

It was ten o'clock when the dryer stopped and I heard a noise in the kitchen someone opening and closing the fridge a cupboard opening and closing then a stool scraping across the floor. The dryer made a ticking sound. It went all quiet in the kitchen so I opened the door between me and it. It was dark in there just a silvery glow I opened the door a bit more and that's when I saw the Master sitting on a stool at the bench Melody's leftovers beside him in front of him his computer phone the silvery glow was from the screen. I stepped into the kitchen I was still in my civvies and gave a little cough. Ah he said the cook. I said I had just finished the evening service I was bowing slightly without meaning to but would he like me to make something for him? This is fine he said pointing to the plate of leftovers and going back to the screen. Let me at least warm it up for you I said. He finally looked up properly like that was the first time he'd actually seen me. Sure he said with a bit of a smile like he didn't care one way or the other but if it made me happy sure. I'll need some light I said. The Master waved his hand at the switch. It was my kitchen I could do what I liked. I turned the lights on over the bench then dimmed them just enough to see but not enough to break the mood. The Master didn't react.

It felt odd in the half-light then in my civvies preparing supper for the Master. I got a pot of water simmering put the plate on top and put a saucepan lid over that. I kept glancing over at him still staring at his phone. A handsome guy once but now grey and a bit balding his skin pale and pasty like a chef's dark rings under his eyes a hangdog look. He knew I was looking at him I could tell by the way he held himself but he didn't look at me. From the fridge I took one of Nick's Stellas uncapped it and put it on the bench. Now he looked up. Why don't you have one yourself? he said. I said no I was working. He watched me for a while then sipping his beer.

Nick and Melody have had an argument I said. You mean Nick and Melody have had another argument he said. They were arguing about me I said Melody doesn't want me here. The Master had to think about this. And you he said do you want to be here? Of course I said why wouldn't I? I tried to say it like I wasn't sure why the Master had even asked. That was good. You came highly recommended said the Master changing tack.

By Head Chef? I asked a bit too quickly. Of course said the Master and he sipped his beer. His phone beeped for a while then he ignored me completely. I got a tea-towel and took the plate off the heat. It didn't look too far off the real thing just a bit grey and tired. The Master put down his phone loosened his tie and took up his knife and fork. I put the plate down in front of him wiped my hands on the tea-towel and started to clean up again.

Do you know how much a bushel of corn is worth he said if I buy it tonight from my trader? I didn't know what he was talking about or even if he was talking to me he might have been talking to his phone. And do you know how much I can sell a bushel of corn for tomorrow into Malawi? Now I knew he was talking to me because he'd even stopped eating to wait for me to turn around before he asked the second question. Well? he said when I was looking at him. Well? I'll tell you he said cutting another piece of lamb and swirling it in the *jus*. Tonight I can buy a bushel of corn from my trader for three dollars twenty US and tomorrow assuming the market holds and chances are with the border troubles it will actually improve by the morning I can sell that bushel to my dealer in Lilongwe for three dollars sixty US. That means I have pocketed forty US cents per bushel of corn. One hundred thousand bushels and I have pocketed twenty-five grand. But why does a big grain trader want to sell their corn to me and let me make a profit? I must have looked like I was interested. Because he said they've got so much corn they don't know what to do with it and if they sold it themselves on the open market without a middle man to put the brakes on that market would get so flooded with corn the price would crash and Malawi could buy it for what it is actually worth which is next to nothing and no-one's going to make any money are they? So how many bushels will we buy Chef? One two three hundred thousand? The Master pushed a few buttons on his phone. A hundred thousand now he said and we'll check the price again before beddy-byes. He smiled. Now *that's* called making money said the Master and he swigged his beer.

He looked exhausted. I kept finding little jobs to make myself look busy. Can I ask you something Chef? the Master said. I was polishing the cutlery. If you had one wish what would it be? I didn't hesitate. To run my own restaurant I said and top the list of the greatest restaurants in the world. It will be called Insouciance I said. The Master smiled he liked someone with ambition I had a little smile too. When I was your age he said let me tell you I only had one wish and that was to be filthy rich well look at me now he said wishes do come true. He smiled again and pushed his finished plate across the bench towards me the knife and fork laid neatly on it. Very nice he said. Trouble is he said I didn't have a clue how much hard work was involved not in getting rich that was easy but staying as rich as the richest you'd been. Now *that* Chef is a challenge. There was a long silence then. The Master looked up at me with a crooked smile a sad smile too I didn't know how to read it. When I smiled back at him I wasn't sure how mine looked either.

Six-forty next morning my mobile beeped. *Spring lamb wagyu rump free-range veal quails.* The house was dark I turned on the desk lamp made some notes had a shower and got dressed there was a soft light at the window the sun just up the pool all glassy the filter humming then my mobile beeped again. *Broad beans runner beans artichokes young leeks.* I wrote some more in my pad and crept quietly downstairs the dog came out through its hatch and sniffed around my ankles then went back in again.

I wasn't in the kitchen long when Mark the tradesman came in a glow of confidence about him bright eyes and healthy skin. Morning Chef he said and he got a carton of milk from the fridge. I'll finish the gazebo this morning he said you should come down and have a look she'll be having breakfast in there soon. Then I start on the new carport and when I've finished that I'll be knocking down the old pergola Deidre doesn't like the grey wood. I've always got something on he said there's always something to do you know how much I make a week he said wiping his milk moustache. I wasn't sure if he meant I should answer. Yeah well don't worry Chef I'd give Ian a run for his money. Supply and demand. If there are more executives and middle managers than a society needs and not enough tradies who's going to be charging top dollar then? He put the milk back in the fridge. Chances are it'll be me and my mates eating out at that restaurant of yours not your Mistress and your Master. He checked his mobile and went outside again.

Quarter past seven I looked into the dining room to see if anyone was there then I went out to check the garden. The Mistress was already out there waiting in her dressing-gown at the wrought-iron table in the morning sun her hair up her make-up done reading a magazine. Have the others eaten she asked when she saw me and I told her no not yet. It's a beautiful day I said. She looked up from the magazine. Yes it is she said. There was a picture of a garden setting just like the one she was sitting in a wrought iron table a sweeping lawn a line of trees. I put the breakfast menu down beside it. And what do you recommend? the Mistress asked. Organic free-range scrambled eggs with truffle oil I said but of course the choice was hers. She looked happy with this. I bowed and went back to the kitchen where Jade was just then walking out with a bowl of cereal I didn't try to stop her. I waited and checked the dining room again. Melody was in there reading the paper I went in and put a menu down beside her then stood back and asked what she'd like. I said I personally recommended the truffled eggs. That sounds nice she said. I went back to the kitchen.

It was not a bad start. When I came out later to clean away the Mistress's dishes she asked what I had planned for the day and I told her I would like to do some more shopping and gave her my list for approval. She read through it then picked up a set of keys off the table and handed them to me. These are for the Prius she said the Master is getting Jade a Volkswagen sports I don't want a cook in my house who can't get what he needs when he needs it. She wasn't looking at me but away off into the garden where down at the gazebo Mark was unpacking his tools. And this she said and she handed me a gold credit card. For a while then I just stood there the Prius keys in one hand the credit card in the other. The Mistress licked a finger and turned the page of her magazine.

I spent a while in my room after that ordering stuff online a long list I won't go into it here but let's just say I covered every base. I paid extra for express. I texted Ray back about the veal then started sketching out the evening menu. *Milk veal five months* said Ray *you won't get better.* Midmorning I let the Mistress know I was heading off now to do the shopping. Just the idea of this made her happy. Yes yes she said and don't forget the bags. She fussed around for a while then looking for the bags.

At Ray's the veal carcass was already on the block and Ray was sharpening his knife when I pushed open the front door and came out the back through the plastic strips. Good morning Chef poked any pork? He was grinning and doing that sharpening thing.

I said I wanted a *sous-noix* to roll and steam in red wine

some free-range quails sweetbreads for tomorrow and more veal neck bones for stock. Ray got to work sharpening his knife. So did you learn any butchering at that school of yours? he said. I told him yes and about what Fabian had taught me then the story of the chops. Ray laughed at that. Never waste a thing he said if you're going to kill an animal make sure it's worth your while. He was stroking the carcass with his free hand the butchering knife in the other. We're all the same when it comes down to it said Ray heads necks shoulders flanks rumps thighs shin feet all flesh and guts and bone there is no part you can't eat. That muscle moves the legs lets the little vealer run that one wags its tail that one there in the neck gets worked when it's crying for its mum. See how I slice that tendon? It seemed to be slicing itself. That cut's good for frying said Ray that one for roasting that one for braising with a *mirepoix*. Don't think you can get away with guessing Chef you need to know them all. Here he said wiping his hands on his apron and handing me the knife a very narrow curved butcher's knife with a worn wooden handle like the one Terry used to use. Go on he said and he watched hands on hips like a father while I ran the knife a few times across the steel and got to work on the hind leg stabbing slicing peeling the muscle away from the bone till pretty soon I had the *sous-noix* cut and trimmed. Good good said Ray that's good.

At Organicasa I bought one handful each of broad beans and young leeks I couldn't believe how fresh they looked like

Marty and Merry had just pulled them out of the ground and a punnet of blueberries to top my *petits fours*. Out the front they had some potted herbs on a stand so I bought them too parsley basil sage rosemary marjoram and thyme. I carried them back to the car in a box. It felt funny all right me loading the stuff into the Prius like that Ray at his back door watching.

Back at the house I unloaded the shopping put it away and set my new herb pots in a row near the back door in the sun. Soon after that a man with a trolley arrived with all the stuff I ordered and I showed him through to the kitchen. He was wearing an orange fluoro jacket and had a pen behind his ear. Chelsea white crockery a lidded frypan a simmer mat aprons napkins side towels garnish banks a larding needle a pastry brush a meat thermometer a *terrine* mould a Thermomix a Magic Freeze liquid nitrogen a blowtorch a dehydrator a vacuum packer an immersion circulator for *sous-vide*. I helped him unload the first lot then he went back to the van for more. Three trolleys twelve boxes all I had to do was sign.

It was nearly lunchtime when I finished unpacking the things the Master came in I hadn't seen him all morning he was on his way to the airport his driver waiting outside. So you've got everything you need? he said then he went out again.

Three o'clock that afternoon I served wine and *canapés* to the Mistress in the new gazebo I didn't need to but I did. You could smell the fresh wood and see the fine sawdust on the ground. The Mistress was in her white smock in front of an easel a palette and paintbrush in her hand. Someone was playing tennis somewhere you could hear the pok-pok of the ball over the fence. I poured a glass of sauvignon blanc and offered the Mistress the tray. She took a *canapé* with one hand held her glass in the other and stepped back to look at her work. I used to draw a lot in the old days she said. She does leaves and flowers mostly. She is having an exhibition soon at the gallery of a friend very big in the charity scene she says perhaps you would like to do the catering? Of course I said bowing. Has the Master gone the Mistress asked and I said yes just before. There was a silence then till Mark started hammering somewhere out the front. I told the Mistress how much I thought her picture looked like the thing she was painting because I figured that's how she sees and she seemed happy with that. Yes she said holding the brush right back close to her ear we all know what a daffodil looks like the skill is to make your painting look like the daffodil we see. I nodded and topped up her glass and caught the drip with my new white napkin.

It was nice down there at the gazebo the lawn the big shady tree the girls not home the house all quiet. The Mistress liked to talk all right but I was there to listen. I stood in the humble position my head at an angle to hear. She asked me again about my family my background all that. I guess she liked knowing I had come from there to here and that she had a hand in it. I answered all her questions. When it was time to go I didn't just turn and leave I made sure I said excuse me I need to go and prepare dinner now she liked me saying that. Walking back across the lawn the big house looming the white apron swishing around my ankles I couldn't help smiling thinking well now how good is this?

That evening she dined alone dressed up this time in a grey and white checked knee-length dress that hugged her a bit too hard. Late that afternoon for a while I'd heard noises in the house Jade coming home from school Melody's high heels on the parquetry floor music upstairs but about six it all went quiet and at seven when I looked into the dining room there was only the Mistress in there.

Roasted quail breast with caramelised onions a rolled *sous-noix* of veal steamed in red wine with buttered broad beans and young leeks and for dessert a plate of *petits fours*. A bottle of Gapstead pinot gris and later a botrytis semillon. The dining table looked huge with just her sitting at it. I put down the plate with the roasted quail breast on it and explained as I did my thoughts about presentation how a round plate for example contains or closes off the meal the eyes going round from twelve o'clock to twelve o'clock but a rectangular plate as here I said on the other hand closes off only the top and bottom and leaves the sides open so we read the meal more like a book. She nodded. The circle I explained is for comfort food warm and reassuring the rectangle for more challenging dishes designed to surprise or unseat the diner. She seemed to follow. The first a red-wine-steamed cut of veal or a slow-braised *osso buco* the second a breast of quail as here or a bar of pressed sweetbread with a smear of truffled veal *jus*. I would demonstrate this tomorrow. She kept calling me *Garçon* and saying other French things I recognised a few and told me how she was travelling with friends next year to a place called Provence. I had a picture in my mind of vineyards and castles and berets I wonder if it is really like that? When I came back into the dining room at the end of the meal to collect the empty plate of *petits fours* the Mistress applauded her hands very flat the fingers very straight the applause echoing in the empty room. *Bravo! Excellent!* she said in French and I gave her a little bow.

So that was the end of my third day here a pretty big day for sure. After I'd cleaned up and put my things in the wash I lay down on the bed upstairs thinking about what I had done and how in such a short time I had managed to set myself up pretty well. I hadn't wasted any time getting my foot in the door now I said to myself I just needed to keep it there.

After that I sat at my desk and started an email to Mum. There were twelve unanswered from her. I explained again why I couldn't come home and how she shouldn't yell at me like that how when Dad died I was waiting at Cook School for Head Chef and how this was very important to me and now she might like to know I was a head chef myself working for a rich family in a really big mansion house. It wasn't like

I could just drop everything and come home just because she said so did she think a career would be waiting for me when I got back? This is the world we live in now Mum I said it's not whether you care it's how crunchy is your pork crackle how pink is your lamb how *al dente* your asparagus spears these are more important than fathers' funerals we can't go to fathers' funerals and still make a success of ourselves. Anyway I said she shouldn't keep nagging I was a big boy now nineteen years of age she needed to let me go. I asked her about Tash and the kids because I felt like I should and whether the new boyfriend Kane had work. It ended up being pretty long that email I must have had things to say. I didn't send it. I started one to Hunter too but I didn't know his address.

For my first Christmas lunch at my new house I did pork with crackling a basted turkey a leg of ham three platters of vegetables four salads seven hundred dollars all up and that was without grog. The Mistress wanted everyone together and somehow she got it. They even wore their paper hats. I wore a Santa hat carved the meat at the table and arranged it on the plates with silver tongs. It was stinking hot. After the plum pudding the Mistress got up and thanked everyone for coming she'd already had one too many. Nick got up too but Melody pulled him down. When I served the turkey I wasn't imagining it Jade leaned right back so I could see down her top.

The days go by pretty easy I've got a good routine now. Breakfast and dinner and in between plenty of time for shopping and prep. Every afternoon about two I have a meeting with the Mistress she gets dressed up for it very formal her hair and make-up done a good dose of perfume all over. I tell her what I'm planning for the evening give her a draft menu and wait for her approval. Sometimes she asks me questions. I don't mind it's the time I get to show off we all need to show off sometimes we're liars if we say we don't. But how will you do this? she'll ask. *Comment ferais-tu ceci*? And I will explain to her how to make say a roast onion powder to sprinkle over a serve of sautéed baby carrots or how to do a strawberry *coulis*. Sometimes her friend Libby joins us. *Qu'est-ce que c'est cet ingrédient là?* Yesterday they both had a big grin. Saturday two weeks from now the Mistress is having her French class over five guests six covers I will do modern French. *Oui oui bien sûr Madame* I said.

Most afternoons Jade's parading by the pool in her red bikini her skin all creamy and pale her butt cheeks perfect like they came out of a mould. All this could be yours Mark says. He has his hands down low near his crotch and keeps looking at me sideways. He's finished the carport and the pergola and started the new extension a gym jutting out from the side of the house below my room where the games room used to be fancy architecture crazy angles a glass wall looking out on the pool. The other morning going out I saw him coming in unloading timber out of his flash green ute. The work car Chef he said I've got two more at home a Prado and a Porsche. Clean overalls every day clean-shaven and shiny his apprentice digs the trenches Mark talks on his mobile phone. We see the Mistress every afternoon in shifts Mark with his architect's drawings me with my evening menu. He's got his stumps and framing timbers I've got my emulsions and powders. I wonder who will be the winner in the end?

Aside from the frenzy of service which now that I am serving the Mistress alone most nights is actually not so frenzied my favourite time is in the evening after cleaning up reading recipes online improving my French making notes in my workbook skimming across the menus of the best restaurants in the world imagining myself in their kitchens. On bits of paper I draw the shapes of plates and sketch out the components of new meals a *tranche* of crispy seared duck's breast say is a dark cross-hatched shape pomegranate seeds are dots my orange and fennel seed emulsion is a random squiggle and last but not least in a black balsamic reduction up along one edge of each plate with a flourish I sign my name.

I spend hours on these sketches lost in my own little world if downstairs they have the patio doors open I can hear the sound of the television and dream myself on it. A Tuesday afternoon show at first then Sunday morning then Saturday afternoon then prime-time Friday evening just me and the camera and the sound guy in my kitchen I will need to learn how to look at the camera. My double-buttoned chef's jacket is opened casually at the top because even though I'm a professional it will be a casual show. I'll give them knife tips and other tips too but don't worry I will always close my eyes when I lean over to smell the aroma from a pan or pot and remind them sincerely that cooking is for pleasure there is no room for agony or angst not on my show anyway.

I cut out recipes too and put them in a folder the really good ones I stick on my wall. The Mistress has been giving me her lifestyle magazines she saw me one day looking so I've got a big collection now. The other night flicking through them I came across this thing about people who'd got out of the city and made a new life on the land. And there he was. With a beard! He was standing next to Rose her belly big holding a chook Hunna ruffling the hair of their oldest kid the other kid his own kid I realised tucked under his arm laughing. Behind them a ramshackle country house pot plants toys and junk on the front veranda a dog with its ears up watching. Hunna was wearing old work clothes long blond hair and a beard he looked shorter than I remember like he was somehow going down into the soil. Rose was wider her bosom and belly big but still that smile a superior smile her hair pinned up a slash of bright red lipstick a hippie cardigan and dress. The photographer wanted a happy healthy family and here they were. I looked for a long while into Hunna's eyes his face tanned his smile open and wide. Past the house behind them I could see a shed then vineyards stretching green towards the hills.

One day while I was working Melody came into the kitchen it was January filthy hot she was in a singlet and shorts. She keeps her own bottle of white wine in the fridge a sticker with her name stuck to the shelf a little Tupperware container of chocolates. I waited before I spoke I wasn't sure I should. I said I hoped it wasn't my fault her and Nick arguing all the time like that. Green eyes she has green eyes I thought they were blue and a little bunch of freckles on her nose. She said don't worry it's not your fault you're just a victim leave it alone.

I said no she'd got it wrong I was not a victim I was happy. She raised a hand at that she really thought I shouldn't have an opinion. I explained to her the idea of service how some people are best equipped to serve wasn't she doing that by going to Cambodia her mother had told me to help the children there?

Melody had a different look now not a nice look she was wondering what this lowly cook was doing talking to her like that let alone about Cambodia. You've got to understand I said that's how society works you've been to university. Melody's green eyes were glaring now they were even a bit red. Please don't dare compare me helping my kids in Cambodia she said to you cooking meals for my stupid mother that is not only insulting but wrong. She had lowered her voice now like the idea of talking to me let alone about humiliation and service was very embarrassing to her. She took her bottle of wine out of the fridge. I started to follow her out I still had things to say but then I thought better of it. I watched her bum swaying while she walked from the dining room into the living room deliberately not looking back. I will cook something special for her I thought something delicate like her freckles a salmon *soufflé* yes that's the thing that will lighten anyone's heart.

That night after evening service I took one up to her room. I knocked so quiet I had to knock three times before she heard I didn't want the others to hear. Come in she said but pissed-off like she thought it was her sister. I stepped in slowly so I wouldn't shock her. She was at her desk with her laptop open a bottle and a glass of wine when she turned around she nearly jumped off the chair. She was in trackpants and a t-shirt now her hair pulled back in a ponytail no make-up her freckles clear.

What do you want? she said like she couldn't see the salmon *soufflé* on the tray in my hands. I held it out towards her. I brought this as a peace offering I said it's a salmon *soufflé* I've been practising it's got fresh Atlantic salmon in it from a recipe by Raymond Thuillier. She looked at me and my salmon *soufflé* it took me a while to realise it was not the *soufflé* that was worrying her but what I meant about it being a peace offering. We had a disagreement I said you thought I should be ashamed. I'm not ashamed but I have come to say I understand why you might have thought that I've tried to see things from your point of view. I never said you should be ashamed she said which made me very happy not because she felt the need to tell me but because now that she was talking to me it had become a conversation. I'm sorry I said but I thought that's what you thought that I should be ashamed to be here cooking for your family that it was beneath me that I should aim higher. No she said I don't think you should feel ashamed but she said it like it was the end of the conversation not the start.

Will you eat my *soufflé* at least I said I made it especially for you. Put it there said Melody pointing to the corner of the desk. I put the *soufflé* down. The page on the screen was for volunteer opportunities in South America. I slid the *soufflé* a little closer to her then carefully with fingers and thumb placed a knife and fork beside it.

I understand your objections Melody I said I'm not going to argue with them all I ask is that while I respect you and what you do you respect me and what I do and that if you don't want to eat in the dining room you will at least allow me to show you the skills I have learnt by letting me serve you here. It is no trouble I don't mind. If you feel hungry and don't feel like coming down to eat with the family all you have to do is text me tell me what you'd like and I'll get something ready for you. I was sort of bowing sideways now trying to get eye contact with her she was looking down at the *soufflé*. Sure she said of course. I think she was trying to get rid of me. Please I said. Yes yes she said I said all right please just let me eat. They were the words I wanted to hear please just let me eat.

Out in the hallway Jade was coming towards me from the pool a white towel around her waist her hair all wet and dripping. I tried not to look but she was looking at me. I smiled and said good evening and went on down the stairs.

For the two weeks running up to the Mistress's French dinner I was very busy I can't tell you first to Ray's to pre-order six corn-fed ducks that I had to salt and prep for *confit* then to Precious Fine Foods to ask Sanjif about Gascony *foie gras d'oie entier*. Yes he said of course he could get it but it would take a week airfreighted and cost three hundred and seventy dollars a kilo. I told him well please what can I say money is no object. He has that thing Indians do with their heads. Of course Chef of course he said. It took me a while to realise how I was actually above him already one rung further up the ladder I mean how I had the shopping power. Good morning Chef he says what would you like today when he comes out from behind the counter bowing. I could learn from Sanjif all immigrants really how do they get rich except by grovelling?

Anyway that Saturday a hot summer's evening the Master away the daughters scarce I already had the table laid and was in my chef's whites cleaned and ironed ready with drinks and *canapés* in the foyer when the Mistress started kissing cheeks at the door. A crispy duck *confit* with an orange and cardamom reduction served with baby spinach salted braised red cabbage crunchy *croutons* and a *porcini vinaigrette*. For entrée Gascony *foie gras d'oie entier* pan-seared with lemon and thyme and for dessert mango *mille-feuilles* with a mixed berry *coulis*. I'd made the *confit* legs the week before but was up half the night worrying myself sick about the wines. In the end I got a mixed case from Sanjif pinot mostly some champagne for starters and to finish a dessert sauterne.

Soon the room was thick with the smell of perfume the women hadn't spared themselves getting dressed the Mistress in a long black body-hugging thing high heels gold necklace and earrings fake tan black eyeliner gold lipstick. I worked the room but not too hard sliding in and out among them back and forth between the dining room and the kitchen with my tray. Each time I approached a new guest the Mistress would introduce me to her in French. Each time I said *bonjour Madame* and each time I gave a little bow. There was not a woman who didn't say ooh.

I couldn't remember all their names but I marked them out in my memory by the colour or style of their hair and clothes. That way I would remember which one drank what and how much and who I was likely to get the biggest compliments from. They were all in their best cocktail dresses mostly black a few red one green their hair fixed up lots of make-up and jewels all of them had had a bit of work done around the eyes. They were all flirting with me more or less but that was all right I was their boy. They went through three bottles of Dom Perignon before I slid up next to the Mistress and asked would they like to take their seats now in the dining room for the serving of the entrée? *Mais bien sûr* she said her eyes alight *oui oui bien sûr*.

First thing on the table when the guests were seated were two bottles of Tuck's Ridge Buckle Vineyard pinot noir a menu on off-white paper with a French café menu border and in front of each guest a little *amuse-bouche* of crisp trout skin salmon caviar and chervil. The room was already full of chatter some French mostly English and plenty of lady-laughter. I called them Madame they called me Chef no-one said *Garçon*.

The *foie gras* got a lot of oohs and ahs and even a little round of applause. I topped up their glasses and left them to it then went back to the mains.

The kitchen for the next half-hour was busy browning off the *confit* legs making the *croutons* salting and braising the cabbage steaming the baby spinach. It was exciting all right the only thing missing was my crew. *Take that back! Do that again! More salt in the sauce!* I had learnt just about everything at Cook School except how to become a boss now I had to learn to boss myself. *Who taught you to carve duck like that!*

Eventually the entrée dishes were cleared and I was ready to plate the mains. I heard the door open and saw the Mistress peeking in. *Excuse-moi* she said I hope you don't mind we'd like to watch the chef at work. The door opened a bit more and the other women crowded in behind pushing her into the room. There were six of them in my kitchen now all clutching their wine glasses craning their necks I did my best to ignore them but at the same time I made sure I absorbed their stares leaning low over the white plates arranging each component according to the sketch blutacked to the cupboard above. Some women asked me questions and I explained. The more technical I made it the more they liked it that's something to remember too. Grab the place above by talking about what those below don't know. But eventually I had to put a stop to it I wiped my hands on my side towel and spoke very firmly to them. Ladies I'm afraid I must ask you to now go back to the dining room and take your places at the table it is time to serve the mains. That was nicely put. They were like school-girls then nudging each other giggling and pushing their way back through the door.

There were more oohs and ahs then when I came back in two plates at a time and put their meals down. The Mistress was first she looked at the plate in front of her then looked up beaming while her guests were served. I had sweated up all right rushing to get everything done and I knew when I leaned over beside them they were smelling my sweat as well as the lardy aroma of the duck and the sweet back-scent of orange and spice. They all had a tingle I could feel it. I opened the Côte d'Or pinot left two bottles on the table turned up the *chansons* and went back to my kitchen.

It was hot in there the oven and all the jets had been on my *mille-feuilles* were prepped and setting in the fridge. I waited a while then looked back through the crack in the dining room door to see if they'd finished their mains. The Mistress was deep in conversation with the woman sitting next to her. I pushed open the door.

Ah! she said when she saw me come in Chef let's have dessert! We're ready for dessert but is dessert ready for us? She was the only one who laughed. Sit down sit down everyone she said even though they were already sitting the chef is bringing dessert! In relays I came back in carrying the *mille-feuilles* a bottle of sauterne and six small stemmed glasses. Put them down put them down said the Mistress she was repeating everything now. I put the last of the things on the table and went back to the kitchen to tidy up. When I thought they were finished I went back in and asked was there anything else? One of them made a joke and all the others including the Mistress put their hands to their mouths.

The strappy leaves in the garden beds were shiny in the moonlight the big front tree was throwing an eerie moon-shadow on the lawn while I stood with my hands clasped in the vestibule the Mistress on the front step calling out her goodbyes the ladies staggering on their heels down the drive to the taxis lined up in the street. *Au revoir au revoir* said the Mistress. I turned and slipped back into my kitchen and spent the next half an hour in there doing my inventory for Monday. When I went back through the dining room into the living room to get the leftover tray of *canapés* I found the Mistress sprawled on the couch a bottle of sauterne in one hand a glass in the other a big coffee-table book open on her lap with pictures of regional French cuisine. Chef! she said when she saw me half-sitting up and trying to hold her balance. A magnificent meal! I am pleased said the Mistress very pleased. She was also very pissed.

Let me tell you she said forcing herself up straight you wouldn't have heard but we were talking about our trip and how we might take a food and wine consultant with us and I can tell you now this idea was very enthusiastically received. Let me tell you Chef it is *you* we were talking about we would like to take *you* with us. She said this last bit with a big wave of her hand so some of the wine splashed up out of the bottle and fell onto the book. You are coming to France with us! she said. Provence! Again the bottle went up and again it splashed into her lap but with this last flourish in one movement holding the sauterne bottle in one hand and her glass in the other she flopped over onto the cushions at the end of the couch. She looked like she was sleeping leaning sideways in one hand the bottle in the other the glass. Her dress had got caught up and the top of her black stockings was showing her face all squished into the cushions one shoe dangling ready to drop.

I wanted to retreat to my room but I felt like I should help so I took the bottle and glass and put them on the coffee table and got down on my knees and got my arms under hers and hoisted her up to nearly standing. She woke up then looked me in the eyes our faces so close they were almost touching. Chef she said. Mistress I replied. I think I may have drunk too much wine she said. I got a better grip. I am sure you will drink less tomorrow I said. That's when I heard a car pull up a door slam and the sound of footsteps on the gravel.

The Mistress kept fluttering her eyes half-open like she was checking I was still there the wine on her breath almost as strong as her perfume. The front door opened it was Melody her keys in her hand a bag over her shoulder. She stopped when she saw us me holding her mother my face turned side-on the Mistress looking at my ear. She flopped her head on my shoulder and buried her face in my neck. Melody I said. But Melody was already putting her keys in her bag and walking upstairs to her room.

The sun goes down early now the evenings are getting cold but I still serve the Mistress in the gazebo most nights with an outdoor heater glowing red and she in her scarves and furs. There is an understanding between us. When I present a degustation as I do sometimes for a surprise she looks at it and says you've read my mind again! She never sends me away she knows I like to watch taking note each time of what she cuts first and how long she looks at it sitting there on the end of her fork. I explain to her where it came from how it got here how it has been prepared she asks me questions and I answer them all sometimes we're out there for hours. I think about Cook School but not too much. Last week browsing my magazines I came across a picture of Head Chef relaxing in the kitchen of his house down the coast a picture of his wife and kids all of them sitting down at a big long table in a light-filled room to eat what he'd prepared. A view out the window of sky and sea. I cut out that picture and blutacked it to my wall.

The Master is away most of the time and when he's not he's locked in his study. If I stop and listen I can hear him in there. I serve the daughters when they text me to their rooms. Melody still looks down her nose at me but every night she eats what I bring Jade is in her last year of school now and home most days studying she texts me too every brunch and dinner and sometimes for supper late. They all come around in the end.

I have asked the Mistress can I have a patch of lawn down past the gazebo to make a vegetable patch and the Mistress has said yes. A test run for Insouciance I said where my kitchen garden will be an integral part of the dining experience fresh produce straight from earth to table with just a little chef's wizardry in between. *Oui oui bien sûr* she said. If I dig it up now and get it mulched and manured it will be producing by next summer. I might even get a few winter crops in. I got Mark to bring the bobcat round and since then I have worked it over in my spare time with a fork and spade. The Mistress likes to watch me from her place in the gazebo but that's OK I don't mind she can watch all she likes.

It's nice out there in the winter sun the loamy smell imagining all the things that will come out of that earth and what I will do with them when they do. The patch is on the lawn down past the big trees good drainage northern sun about three metres square. I have divided it in five like the garden at Cook School and will rotate it the same. Last week the first seeds arrived in a packet in the post next full moon I will start planting broad beans spinach spring onions carrots and on the fallow ground a legume crop.

The family has been watching. The other day I saw the Master standing up there near the back door looking down at me past the trees. The Mistress came up beside him to explain. The girls too. So this live-in cook is not some fly-by-night whim of their mother's they are thinking this is serious he is here to stay. I have taken a leaf out of Mark's book. Why shouldn't I live off this house for a couple of years watching learning growing so when I'm done and Insouciance is opened I can sit back smiling and watch all those people ringing the number begging my maitre d' to please pretty please get them a table please. No Sir Madam I'm sorry we are booked out a year in advance. White walls white tablecloths skylights light wells galleys and platforms hydroponic lighting in the centre a pomegranate tree and garden beds divided into rows. A little Asian kid in a coolie hat tilling the soil lifting baby carrots on orders from the kitchen and carrying them in his wicker basket to a Commis Chef waiting at the fountain beside the door a rusty old garden tap pouring water into a rusty old bucket a trick of the eye the plumbers have done it this is where the vegetables are washed. The customers watch all this they are in awe here's something they've never seen before they'll be able to tell their friends. The Commis Chef takes the carrots and disappears into the kitchen. The family up at the house are watching just like my diners will.

The other night after I hadn't heard from her for a while I went up to Melody's room. I kept knocking but there was no answer. Jade came out of her room one door down. What is it? she said meaning the plate in my hand. Grilled red mullet I said with a celery root *mousseline*. I don't like celery she said. She was wearing pink trackpants and a sloppy white t-shirt. Where is Melody? I asked but Jade just went back inside. I waited till she was gone then turned the handle I could feel the hollow echo even before I looked in.

The bed was there the cupboard and drawers but all Melody's bits and pieces were gone. I had a picture of her in my mind her hair pulled back in a ponytail t-shirt and jeans a bunch of Cambodian orphans around her. I turned around the fish was getting cold I would take it back down to the kitchen but then the Mistress was standing in the doorway. You can have it if you like she said with one of her smiles. I thought she meant the fish then I realised she was talking about the room. Melody has gone away indefinitely she said. I told her I was happy with my little room upstairs and really there was no need. No she said I insist you have done your time you have been with us how long you are one of the family now. Why leave a nice room like this empty she said while you are living up in the attic? Go and get your things. I bowed and the Mistress moved aside but not enough to stop me brushing past her on the way.

It didn't take long to move my things I shoved what I could in my daypack carried my uniforms down then went back for my magazines my workbook my Larousse my knives in the old red tea-towel my clock my truffle in a jar. When

I came down that time Jade had changed she was in a short skirt and black top now standing in her doorway watching me go in. I put everything away it felt weird all right knowing Melody's stuff had been in there then last I brought down my computer and printer and set them up on the desk near the window. The Mistress came back with sheets and pillowcases and put them on the end of the bed. Fresh linen she said then she went away again.

I opened the curtains and looked out. It was a different view across the front garden to the street the light out there making a halo around the trees. There was even a little balcony I went out to get some air. I could see the lights from Jade's room further along and hear music coming from it. The Master's car pulled into the drive and the headlights went off. I ducked down and waited till I heard his footsteps on the gravel and the front door open and close.

Later on my way back from the bathroom before bed I saw his study door open and a light spilling out into the hall. When I slowed down to look the Master looked up. Hello I said I'm sorry I'm just on my way back to my new room. Come in he said come in. I stepped inside I wasn't sure what to think. Sit down he said sit down there was a chair in the corner I pulled it up beside him. His computer screen was huge he had at least half-a-dozen windows open with columns and figures flashing a row of clocks down one side showing the time in London Hong Kong New York.

I leaned forward it was mesmerising. Every now and then the Master would tap the keyboard or click the mouse and sometimes let out a sound of disappointment or surprise. He had some music going nineties pop and was eating cashew nuts from a bowl. What's your thing he said what do you like? I didn't know what he meant I was just sneaking back to my room I still had tomorrow's menus to do. I mean what commodity do you like he said you're a cook you must have a favourite something? Apples strawberries salt chocolate coffee? I'll give you a grand he said. Sugar's just gone down that's a good buy now. Refined or unrefined? Unrefined I said. A grand's worth of unrefined sugar said the master at eighty-nine cents a kilo. He clicked his mouse and leaned towards the screen.

It was nice all right sitting there at the Master's elbow I bet Mark the tradesman never sat in the Master's study eating cashews watching the figures dance on the screen. You've got to understand son said the Master it's all a game but it's games like these that grease the wheels I'm a money-maker not a thing-maker and I'm not the only one. It's a big club he said and I'm very happy to be a member. It was true he did look happy every other time I'd seen him he looked exhausted distracted like he was carrying the weight of the world on his shoulders but here in his study in front of his computer with his music on and his cashew nuts he looked happy and alive.

Swings and roundabouts said the Master that's how things go I make in the night what I lose in the day. Soybean derivatives going down yes we'll have some of that. He clicked his mouse watched and waited then leaned back in his chair. With one hand he pointed behind him without looking towards a tall set of shelves in the corner. Grab that bottle of whisky he said and a couple of glasses you drink whisky don't you? I said I did even though I didn't. I got the bottle and two glasses. On the other shelves were knick-knacks trinkets he'd bought on his travels a couple of golf trophies framed pictures of his family he and the Mistress when they were young the Statue of Liberty behind them and a shot of the two daughters pushing in close and smiling their perfect smiles. There was a fine crack in the plaster from the ceiling down the wall to the edge of the window frame.

I put the bottle on the desk and the Master poured us each a glass. Now I'm really in it up to my neck I thought. I heard a toilet flush somewhere further down the hall then the next thing the Mistress was in the doorway in her dressing-gown. Oh she said the boys are having a little party. Don't keep him up all night love she said and she pulled the door closed and went away. She looked different without her make-up like one of those hairless dogs. Don't worry about her said the Master she doesn't have a clue. I wasn't sure what he meant I wasn't going to ask.

I stayed another two hours in the Master's study watching the figures on the screen in the end I never really understood what he did. After two hours he told me he was back in the black leaning in his chair a bit flushed from the whisky and by the looks of it very happy with himself. He checked his watch a big chunky watch and said all right one for the road? It was awkward but I had to excuse myself I stood up and explained how I had to get the menus ready for tomorrow.

The Master looked at me probably for the first time he hadn't taken his eyes off the screen. You don't need to do all that crap he said if it's only Deidre eating. He meant doing everything involved in getting a first-class meal on the table. I told him it wasn't just the Mistress and that in fact most nights and often the days now I had been feeding Jade and Melody too. It was not a duty I said it was a pleasure. A chef is not just a cook but an artist and an artist I said is someone who above all should aim to make a lasting impression. It gives me pleasure I said to prepare an attractive well-balanced perhaps even surprising menu and deliver what is promised onto the plate. I am only here to serve.

The Master nodded but he wasn't listening he was clawing at the mouse again and watching something on the screen. Yes he said you do what you need son it's all going down the shitter anyway. He leaned very close to the screen then reached into his pocket and took out a wad of money. He glanced down long enough to peel two fifty dollar notes off it and hand them over to me. There's your profit he said. He said that last bit like there was nothing else to say.

One morning in the garden turning over my legume crop a frost on the ground a chill in the air I noticed for the first time how things had gone quiet on the building site up at the house. I hadn't seen Mark for days. The footings had been poured the first framing timbers up but then it had just stopped. I went up to have a look. It was a big project all right. The games area directly below my old attic room had been completely demolished and opened out on two sides in one direction towards the pool and the other towards the garden. When it was finished the new gym and spa area would be a whole new wing. You could have trained an army in it. I stood there looking at it all empty and quiet the faint smell of concrete and wood. I heard voices down the side Mark the tradesman and another guy talking. The digging had weakened the foundations they were saying they'd need to get someone in. Mark had a mate he said they'd add it to the bill. I heard them walking back to their cars their feet crunching on the gravel the low grumble of Mark's custom ute. Later when I went back to my new room I saw for the first time the crack in the plaster just like in the Master's from the cornice on one side right across the ceiling to the other.

I was still standing staring at it when my mobile beeped it was Jade texting me for something sweet. I went to the kitchen and made a strawberry *soufflé*. When I came back up later her door was open and she was sitting on the bed with a laptop on her knees trackpants a white singlet no bra her hair pulled back. I could hear the Master tapping away in his study so I was very careful with the volume of my knock. Come in she said. I put the tray down on the bedside table eyes front and centre. Strawberry *soufflé* I said. She dug the spoon in and drew it out she wasn't looking at me. I know you like my sister she said do you miss her? Her chin was up all haughty the spoon dripping red. I don't like anyone Jade I said I am only here to serve. That's not true she said turning to me that's a dirty rotten lie. She put the *soufflé* in her mouth and let it melt then pulled the spoon out and licked it. You know you can have me she said. I was listening so hard to the sounds from the study that my ears had started to ring. But you don't want me do you said Jade in fact you don't know what you want. I want to open my own restaurant I said and debut in the top ten that is my only want. Jade wrinkled her nose at that and gave a little snort. Her nipples were showing through her singlet she pushed her shoulders back. Anyway I said sorry Jade but I have things to do. I could feel her eyes on me as I went.

That afternoon I heard the Mistress talking to someone at the front door at one point his voice very loud. It was Nick. Ah he said coming into the kitchen the chef's still here still sucking on the teat! He'd been drinking all right his forehead red a psychotic look in his eye. The Mistress was standing in the doorway she didn't know what to do. So you've still got your boy Deidre he said he's a good boy isn't he? How old are you now boy? He was talking to me. Nineteen I said twenty next month. Nineteen he said and this is the best you can do? He waved an arm around the room. He was hunting me down that was the reason he was here he'd left the Mistress behind now eyes only for his prey. He stood up next to me and put his face close. I could smell the grog on his breath. When I was nineteen he said I was already running my own business he turned around to check that fact with the Mistress then turned back to me again. Why haven't you got ambition like that? I explained to him softly how I did have ambition my ambition was to run my own restaurant which I hoped to do one day soon.

And will I get a table there? Nick asked. Well I said I don't know the prices won't be cheap. Nick thought that was hysterical. He threw back his head looked at the Mistress and laughed. He staggered backwards for a bit. The Mistress looked embarrassed. But you know what Nick said coming right up close again let me tell you something you might get your own restaurant Chef but you're still never going to catch me. Never. Never ever. Because by the time you're doing that boy I'll be CEO of a publicly listed company pulling a million a year. You get it? It doesn't matter *what* you do Chef you'll *always* be behind. Please Nick said the Mistress that's enough now please. Nick had got pretty heated all right he was spitting while he spoke. No I said keeping my face right up close to his that's true I will never catch you but if it all goes well one day I'll be on the telly.

The word telly hung there in the air for a while the next thing happened fast. Nick whacked me with an open hand hard across the back of the head. Please said the Mistress. When he saw how I didn't react he hit me again and again. My head just sort of jerked each time and bounced back on its spring. Oh don't do that Nick please said the Mistress but weakly like she was talking to a kid poking a snail with a stick. It's not his fault Nick he's just the cook please Nick leave him alone. Jade was in the doorway now watching. Nick whacked me a couple more times like he needed to finish the job then he gave his hand a shake. He's a dickhead Deidre he said turning around brushing past her to the door watch out for him I'm telling you one day that little fuck will suck you dry. Jade stepped aside to let him go. The Mistress looked at me there was nothing she could do her face was like the face of one of those people who've just dropped their groceries in the street.

Later in the gazebo under a late-winter sun the scene in the kitchen still hanging in the air the Mistress asked could she draw me. I want to do a study of the chef at work she said. I think she was trying to comfort me. She's doing life-drawing but for the moment she has me with my uniform on. I'm holding a whisk in my hand. She asks me to furrow my brow. What are you thinking? she says. I don't tell her about my sore head or my ugly thoughts of revenge but that I am imagining doing a mousse working the mixture at just the right speed so it will emulsify not separate. The Mistress is happy with this. Yes she says sharpening her pencil. It is a nice day outside cold but clear and with the angle of my head as I whip my imaginary mousse I can see my vegetable garden down there past the trees the winter peas high on their frames.

When the Mistress was finished I put on some old clothes grabbed the spade went down to the garden and marked out another six square metres of lawn. I dug like crazy her watching from the patio it was late when I walked back dirty sweaty and sore to the house. I had a shower but before I went down for evening prep I got on the computer and looked around for more seeds everything I would need ready for spring one month away carrots radishes turnips swedes lettuce spinach rocket sorrel tomatoes capsicums eggplants zucchinis. While this is my kitchen and I am their cook there will always be food on the table.

It was about a month after that and I was taking supper to Jade's room one night when I heard someone talking in the Master's study. It took me a while to realise who it was. I stood near the door so I could just see in. The Master was at his desk I could hear him talking and her talking back had she come home without me knowing? Please Melly the Master was saying his voice soft like he didn't want anyone to hear it will make your mother happy. I'll pay don't worry grab a quick flight back stay with us a few days and you'll be back there with your kids for New Year's. It went quiet then for a while until Melody answered. The Master turned the volume down I had to strain to hear. Do you really think I'm going to come home for Christmas to that fucking madhouse she was yelling and sit down and eat a meal that creepy cook has made like it's some sort of normal fucking thing to do? Please Melly said the Master. You make me sick all of you said Melody here I am trying to give these poor kids a decent meal a decent life and there you are sitting on your fat arses like the fat capitalist pigs you are. And where's my money she said you said you were going to send it two weeks ago you promised me where is it? Melly darling please said the Master I sent you ten grand already. Melody screamed something then but I didn't catch it the Master flicked the volume off and slumped back in his chair. I pushed the door open a bit to see. Melody was still screaming at him her tanned face all ugly and contorted looking right down into the camera no make-up her hair up in a ponytail just like I thought. The Master was sitting way back in his chair now clutching his drink trying not to look he reached out and touched the keyboard and I saw the screen go blank. My mobile was vibrating in my pocket. *Where are you where's my supper?* it said.

I hadn't heard anything from Organicasa all week so this morning I went down to see. A fortnight till my second Christmas and I am organising a big menu to impress. You will eat with us this year the Mistress had said you are part of the family now. There was a sign on the door thanking their customers for their support but saying that due to circumstances beyond their control they'd had to close the business. A smiley face at the bottom. I put my nose to the window and looked in all the shelves and display units empty a sad and lonely-looking thing. I tried to remember what vegetable went where what I had coming on in my garden and whether I'd get by. At Ray's the bell rang but he didn't come out I had to open and close the door a few times and yell. Come through he said but grumpy. He had a Kurobuta pig on the block and was sharpening his knife. And you just want a bit of belly? he said. I told him I was practising for Christmas. Diced pork belly braised with herbs wrapped in caul fat sautéed and finished in the oven you got my caul fat didn't you? Ray made out like he didn't hear he put down his butcher's knife and picked up a cleaver and with one almighty whack he took off the pig's head. Yes I got your caul fat he said it's in the tub over there he kept hacking at the forequarters slapping them down one at a time sharpening his knife again.

What's wrong I said did I do something wrong? Ray stopped his hands already bloodied. It's not you he said it's not your fault you're just a little cog in the machine. No he said sharpening his knife again the blade singing on the steel my mistake I should have stayed with my kind. I didn't know what he was talking about. We've got to know our place he said these people are better than us they're smart we're dumb. I gave him the look that let him know I didn't know what he meant.

My old man was a butcher said Ray and his old man before him I'm from a long line of butchers all from crap-poor suburbs but of all those butchers I'm the only one who ever made it to the centre do you understand what I mean? It's only me that made it and that's all history remembers you for son. But of course I'm not *from* the centre am I? I'm a commuter like the rest of us everyone's a commuter except you maybe he said smiling. That's the way the customers like it. They don't want to think I'm living here among them at night with my sharp knives and butcher's thoughts. When that bell rings and that customer walks in it doesn't matter what I'm doing what I'm thinking having a shit whatever when I wipe my hands and go out through those plastic strips I'm Ray's Fine Meats I've got my good face on I'm ready to give them whatever they want everything but a shoulder massage or a little rub down there.

Ray stopped sharpening his knife and stood staring at the carcass on the block in front of him. Then holding the knife like a dagger he started hacking at it. I couldn't do anything but watch and hope he got my pork belly out of there without ruining it it would be minced pork the way he was going. I've got to give up my spot he said what can I do I'm going back to the caryards and powerlines to sell chops and sausages in the mall. And once you go out there son you don't come back you only get one shot at it everyone knows that. I've worked ten years flat out at this I'm out of bed and in the car every morning six days a week before dawn and back on the freeway home every evening after dark. I only see my house in the daylight once a week on Sunday when I go out for a few hours in the afternoon to fiddle with my orchids. And for what? To hold my spot here in the richest leafiest suburb where people pay thirty dollars a kilo for lamb backstraps to give to their cat and why?

To make money I said to value-add to increase your margin and that way your profit. Ray thought that was the funniest thing he'd ever heard he backed away from the block waving the knife in front of him like he was saying no no please go away you crack me up his fat belly was shaking with laughter. But isn't that what you're doing I said marking up your product taking advantage of the buying habits of your customer that's what I'll be doing in my restaurant that's what we're supposed to do. Ray stopped laughing and looked at me. He wiped a hand across his mouth.

Yes yes that's what we're supposed to do but here's the catch son here's the catch. *What if they don't pay their bills?*

Ray let the idea hang in the air between us then he went back to butchering what was left of the pig sliding the knife along the backbone chopping down hard through the ribs. He said the next bit without looking at me like maybe it was all too shameful for him. I'm going to the wall Ray said I've got lots of customers who haven't paid their bills for months some haven't paid for years. I've taken out loans another one last week but the bank won't do it anymore. But can't you just remind them I said that they haven't paid maybe they've just forgotten? Ray looked hard at me. Get your head out of your arse son he said I'm a shitkicking butcher from a shitkicking suburb I'm lucky to be here what right have I got to ask these people to pay their bills? Do you think when they come in here for their special piece of meat they want to hear me banging on about them paying their bills would you ask them to pay their bills would you have the balls for that? Of course not you're a fuckin' eunuch just like me.

See this he said and he slapped the pig's rump onto the centre of the block. And this? He was holding a meat tenderiser by the hammer end. Lesson one today son and don't forget it every day they fuck you. He put the tenderiser handle into the arsehole of the pig and shoved it in and out a few times looking at me with a blank expression like he was saying see? He took the handle out with a plop and threw it on the block wiped his hands on his apron picked up his knife and started sharpening it again. That's good you're fucking the daughters he said without looking at me I hope you're doing them from behind because that cunt Ian is sure as hell fucking you.

Ray worked for a while quietly then chopping the hind-quarters into knuckle ends hocks trotters he pushed them all aside pulled one of the big loins back in front of him and started cutting through the ribs to get the belly. He seemed calmer now. He took the belly off a beautiful-looking piece of meat nice even layers of fat trimmed it up and pushed it across the block towards me. There you go he said take it it's yours but use it wisely son because it's the last thing you're getting on account. I looked at him not believing. No more credit he said.

But the Fletchers are paying their bills I said surely they're paying their bills? I haven't seen a cent from them for the past nine months said Ray and I don't expect to see any either. And don't look at me like that he said of course I'm not going to ask them for the money I tried to bleed these people dry and now they're bleeding me. But no more credit you hear me he said if you want meat from me from now on you're bringing cash. And no mates' rates he said you pay top price like everyone else I've told all the house cooks that. Now said Ray wiping his hands and picking up my pork belly let's get this grubby little deal over and done with.

He walked back out into the shop put the belly on the scales took note of the weight and the price then wrapped it up and stuck one of his little black and gold seals on the front. When he put the package up on the counter he didn't say thank you have a nice day he just opened the accounts book on the bench and wrote our last line in it. I could see his face in the mirror very determined but somewhere behind too it a soul sad and defeated.

When I got back to the house the Mistress was in a flap. She'd been talking about the French trip but now she said the Master wanted to move the whole family there. For business reasons she said. We are going to get a villa down south! She wanted me to go with them she'd already discussed it with the Master. I said I wasn't sure I'd got used to my kitchen here. But we will build you a new kitchen there said the Mistress you will have everything you need just like in the magazines! There will be grapevines and herbs we will cycle to the village for bread!

That morning late Jade texted me for breakfast I made a pancake stack with maple syrup and took it up to her room. The door was open she was at her desk in her undies and singlet it was hard for me not to look her legs crossed her thigh all shiny and stretched. Later around twelve back down in the kitchen she sent me another and asked could I bring something else? I made a fresh vegetable frittata and when I went up this time she was on the bed but I was strong and focussed. I put the plate down beside her. Vegetable frittata I said no lactose very healthy. Later I heard her in the shower but by then I was at my desk working on my supply problems thinking it all through concentrating hard.

Then that evening the mains served the Mistress on her own in the dining room me cleaning up and putting things away she appeared like out of nowhere. She'd come the back way through the laundry door no-one ever came that way tight jeans a red crop-top her cream belly showing red lipstick black eyeliner and a look that spelled trouble. She dipped a wet finger into the little bowl of rose salt on the bench. Have you got any wine? she said. There was a half-bottle of pinot opened. I poured a glass and handed it to her. She held it up close to her mouth her eyes darting sideways shivering like she was cold.

If you want your restaurant I can talk to my dad she said you know he'll do anything I ask. She sipped the wine and looked at me. Thank you Jade I said I appreciate your concern as you know I can't stay here forever I will need to move on eventually. If you can have a word with him yes. She stepped towards me cocked her head to one side and turned her face up to mine. You're not going yet though are you? she said. There was nothing I could do. Her mouth right there her eyes slowly closing and next thing I know I am kissing her on the lips. We kissed like that for a long time her hands on my back me holding her maybe a bit too hard till I heard the Mistress calling out *Chef! Chef!* I peeled Jade off grabbed a fresh bottle of red put a white napkin over my arm and went into the dining room where the Mistress was sitting up waiting. When I came back out Jade was gone.

I couldn't stop my hands from shaking my skin had gone

all hot and sweaty I took off my apron and went outside the moon just up a big yellow moon against a deep dark sky and took some gulps of air. Back in the kitchen I worked like a madman pulling everything out of the fridge the freezer the cupboards making an inventory of what I had. The Mistress stood in the doorway watching with a glass of wine in her hand. Later outside in the moonlight I made a list of my vegetables too.

That night in my room my head still buzzing I sat at my desk and wrote an email. It was the one I'd always meant to write since that day at Cook School when my sister didn't come. It came out like a vomit. Dear Tash yes it's me you asked so I'll tell you that guy I cut what started it all he bashed me put me down his girlfriend watched and made out like I was a pig how's that feel pig he said so don't get on your high horse sister sitting there in your McMansion and tell me what I done was wrong I've seen wrong I know wrong awful wrong who are you to judge? I thought about it for a while but in the end I didn't send that one either.

Next night walking through the empty dining room I heard a voice I swore I recognised it coming from the other side of the door. I stopped to listen. It was Head Chef all right there was no doubt about it Head Chef was in the living room talking to the Master. I opened the door to look.

It felt like a dream. He had grown bigger in my mind but now in reality through the crack in the door he actually looked very small. He was sitting on the couch the Master in his armchair opposite between them on the coffee table a bottle of Margaret River cabernet sauvignon. I could see the label from there. Head Chef was leaning forward he'd hardly touched his glass using his hands to plead with the Master about something. The Master was sitting back in his armchair one hand on the arm the other holding his glass looking there was no other way to put it down his nose at Head Chef. I couldn't quite catch what Head Chef was saying he was talking very fast but then he started to raise his voice and the Master sat back. What I heard next was what I'd always known I'd hear but that didn't mean I wanted to hear it.

But I've helped you all I can the Master was saying I've bailed you out three times already I've got my own problems too. Head Chef put his head in his hands. What can I do mate said the Master I can't keep throwing good money after bad. But I'm rationalising said Head Chef looking up I've closed Dubai I'm closing Sydney I've pulled the pin on Singapore I'm turning Melbourne to bistro I can trade my way out of this Ian I know I can. You said that last time said the Master. Not my fault said Head Chef not my fault. What about your Asian mates said the Master what happened to them? Head Chef went silent. We've all got to trim our sails said the Master you can't keep selling to the high end when the high end's gone broke. I know mate said Head Chef in a pitiful tone I fuckin' know. You've got to cut your losses the Master was saying I'm not the only investor who's gone cold on this stuff I'm changing my portfolio to property. But you were there from the start said Head Chef you gave me your commitment. Things have changed said the Master and he leaned right back in his chair as if to say haven't I already made that clear? There was a silence then. Drink your wine said the Master for chrissakes it cost me a hundred dollars a bottle. Head Chef looked up I couldn't see his face but I hoped that made him smile.

There was a sound then keys in the front door and footsteps in the foyer the Master and Head Chef sat up their glasses in their hands and that's when the Mistress entered. She was coming back from her French class she couldn't help it *bonjour Monsieurs* she said. The Master smiled. Head Chef gave her a little wave. It took her a while to take off her heels. But don't let me disturb you gentlemen she said a shoe in each hand has anyone seen the cook? The Master shook his head. The Mistress headed off upstairs and the two men waited till she was gone.

You've still got the cook said Head Chef don't forget I gave you him. Yeah said the Master and I think he's fucking my daughters. That shut Head Chef up. But he was the best I had said Head Chef I didn't have to give him to you surely that counts for something? The Master thought this question was beneath him he sat right back in his chair this time like he was getting as far as away from this begging dog as he could.

Head Chef read the signal picked up his glass and downed it then filled again it from the bottle.

Listen mate said the Master leaning forward you've got to understand my hands are tied. We were all taking risks and sure it's people like us taking risks that keeps this country going that's what those other cunts will never understand but sometimes mate I'm sorry you've got to cut your losses. Sometimes a risk comes off and sometimes it doesn't fuck knows how you tell. But I'm going to lose the lot Ian the fucking lot the beach house everything you've got to help me I just need a little something to get me over the hump. Sorry mate said the Master I don't know much but if you want my advice start a soup kitchen that's where we're heading buddy the whole thing's gone to shit. But I've got a wife and kids said Head Chef. So have I said the Master. I've got a reputation said Head Chef. The Master didn't answer that. They both sipped their wine and stared at a spot on the coffee table.

I could see Head Chef in half-profile now his hair all askew his face covered with grey stubble. He had his hands clamped between his knees wringing them together. Even from that distance through the crack in the door I could see they were no longer chef's hands there were no cuts no burns no calluses they were the doughy hands of a patron. I remembered those same hands plating that lamb drizzling the *jus* gesturing palms up to the finished dish virtuoso hands but now the Master was talking again. Listen mate we've got to wind this up don't be offended but here's an idea. You're a famous chef he said you're one of our best you've got your own telly show you're a celebrity. The Master lowered his voice I had to open the door a bit more to hear. Sell your story he said. Get yourself an agent. Poor boy from bad suburb climbs his way up goes overseas works under all the big chefs gets his arse kicked around the kitchen falls over gets up borrows money opens a little restaurant back home debuts in the top ten opens another marries a model gets his own TV show expands the empire overseas. But the dream turns sour people give fine dining the flick he closes his restaurants goes into debt it looks like there's no way out. But he hasn't given up he says no way I won't let go of the dream. He works for charity projects plans a comeback does the Kokoda Track he's going to rebuild don't you worry. Pictures of you and the missus and the kids in a community garden somewhere picking vegies. With a good agent mate you're looking at two hundred grand minimum.

The Master was pretty excited about his idea but Head Chef had slumped back into the couch now his body all limp. Well? the Master was saying. Head Chef took a while to answer. It's a good idea mate said Head Chef I'll think about it for sure but what he was really thinking was that from this house today he would be leaving empty-handed.

The Mistress was coming down the stairs again she'd put her flat shoes on. I can't find him anywhere she was saying he's planning a hare though I saw the menu on his desk hare darling did you teach him that? Head Chef smiled at her. He's a star said the Mistress an absolute star. She was crossing the living room now towards the dining room. Have you seen him love? she said to the Master but he just shook his head. She was coming straight towards me I couldn't believe what I'd heard I stepped away from the dining room door pulled it closed and scurried back into the kitchen so by the time the Mistress came in I was in my apron whisking some eggs.

That night in my room I took out the hundred dollars the Master had given me from my sock drawer and next morning I went down to Ray's and bought a side of lamb with cash. He was only open three days now Wednesday Thursday Friday he was his usual grumpy self. North-east Victorian grain-fed six weeks finished off with hay and water eleven kilos per side dressed weight he charged me sixty dollars the side. I figured I'd get a month's worth of meals out of it butchering it myself and serving lamb say every few nights. I asked Ray could I use his knife and he stabbed it into the block. Don't look at me like that I said I know what I'm doing. I'm not going to end up selling forequarter chops and sawdust sausages to fat losers in the mall I'm going to be smarter than that. I picked up the knife and stabbed it into the flesh and started dismembering the lamb. And what happens when your money runs out said Ray what are you going to do then?

The pool's got no water. Some men with a machine came and emptied it out because of the cracks all that's left down the deep end is a bit of black liquid and leaves. Yesterday I saw the Master out there pacing up and down talking hands-free on his mobile at one point stopping very sudden and staring down into the hole. I could see the Mistress watching from behind the patio doors. She was staring into a hole too.

I clean Ray's three mornings a week it's not a bad routine. He pays me in meat. I park the Prius in the carpark just before dawn and use the spare key to open up. It's quiet in there the faint smell of detergent from the night before the front window the display cabinets empty. It's my job to give the glass a good clean bring out the trays of meat and put fresh garnish on them. After I'm done I choose what I want weigh and price it myself and leave a chit on the register keys. Twelve dollars worth max. Lamb cutlets a small rolled roast a free-range chicken a packet of quails some marbled rump pigs' trotters some sweetbreads duck livers lean mince.

This morning when I turned the key I couldn't believe it the shop was stripped the cupboards empty the register and scales gone the coolroom empty except for the big wooden chopping block in the middle. In the centre of the block Ray had stabbed his old butchering knife into a note. *Bend over* it said. It was not until the sky had lightened that I saw the big piece of butcher's paper sticky-taped to the front window. I went out to read it. Ray thanked his customers for their loyalty but said he needed to spend more time with his family. False and friendly to the end. I went back inside to look for the account book but of course he'd taken that too. I checked the switchboard the power was still on I turned on the switch for the coolroom there was a clunk then a hum. That night after dinner I got on the computer and searched around till I found a place a farm just out past Wallan eighty minutes round trip seven dollars petrol tops. They would do live lambs thirty kilo liveweight a hundred and sixty-two dollars each veal two-fifty kilo liveweight six hundred and twenty dollars each pigs ninety kilo four hundred and ninety dollars. While I had the key and the shop was empty I'd bring them back to Ray's slaughter and butcher them there and keep the meat in the coolroom. I heard a car pull up below I stood out of the light and watched. It was Jade on her way out all dressed up her hair all shiny a handbag with a fat gold chain. She got into a dark Mercedes sports with a guy behind the wheel. I knew she knew I was looking.

They wobble like jelly you can't keep them still and when they see the knife they start squealing. The farmer a scrawny guy with a flannel shirt and goatee beard helped me get the pig into the back seat of the Prius and buckle the belts around it. He trussed its legs tore a strip of rag and tied it tight around its snout. I could hear it huffing all the way down the highway.

I'd found that room the day before in the far east wall of the wing under my old attic room near where they'd started the extension. I always thought it was the pump room for the pool. I was chasing a chook that had got out of its pen and saw the door a little bit open so I pushed it all the way. Bicycles computers monitors keyboards printers copiers TVs recorders speakers microwaves coffee machines pasta makers bread makers sandwich grills deep fryers exercise bikes treadmills all thrown in there one on top of the other a room full of what this family called junk. I got a hundred and ten for the Shogun hybrid three-sixty for the Samsung LCD thirty for the LG microwave and twenty for the sandwich grill.

The sun was just up when I got the pig out of the back seat and led it on a rope through the empty carpark in through the back door of Ray's. I took the rope and muzzle off and let it wander around the shop for a while to calm it down then I shooed it back through the plastic strips.

It was different from a lamb a big blubbery thing impossible to get hold of in the end I sat on its back riding it like a horse and leaned down with my arm tight around its neck Ray's butchering knife in my hand. It started shaking and squealing I hoped to christ no-one would hear I ran the knife across its throat and sliced down hard and kept slicing till it stopped. When it keeled over which actually took a while it took me over with it so next thing I was lying on my side still holding on the legs kicking can-can the blood all up my knife arm and over my shirt and spreading in a big pool on the floor. You idiot I thought the pig half-lying on me bleeding onto the floor I could have done that recipe for *boudin noir* Normandy-style with cooked apples and a squeeze of lemon.

I was still lying there thinking how many blood sausages I would have got when I realised the pig had stopped moving. There was no way I could hoist it up onto the block on my own so I did the first bit of butchering down there on the floor. I got the head off blades loin legs and hung them each on hooks then lifted the big middle bit up onto the block. I was happy there in the quiet just the sound of the knife slicing tendon and flesh and the occasional zing of it on the steel imagining all the recipes I would do. It's a good life the chef's life every day different every meal a challenge a creative life. Take that I said you losers with each cut of that pig and you I said to my Head Waiter table one the famous actor and his wife. Take that I said and that.

Later that morning I was wheeling the big esky up the front steps of the house with my selected pork bits in it when the Mistress passed me going out. Jade's not feeling well she said could you make a pot of chicken soup and take some up to her room? I said of course and waited on the top step till she was gone. In the kitchen I parked the esky in the corner looked around in the fridge and found the chicken carcass I'd kept for stock right up the back. When I took the soup up later Jade was in bed the strap of her white singlet falling off one shoulder. She asked me to put the tray in her lap. It wasn't my imagination I know when I put it down she sat up close to me her warm breath on my neck. I let myself hover there for a minute a strand of hair touching my shoulder. It's chicken soup I said leaning back it will do you good there's more there if you want.

She was looking at me trying not to look. Did you do it with Melody? she said. No I said. And what about my mum? No way I said no. She had her legs open under the doona her eyes half-closed staring past me towards the window. I bowed and backed away.

Down in the kitchen I sorted my pork bits into cuts vacuum-packed and labelled them and put them in the fridge then my mobile beeped. Upstairs this time the sun had moved and was bright on the wall behind her she was wearing her white singlet and undies her legs already open. She didn't wait she pulled the singlet up over her head her breasts smooth like curds come on she said and before I knew it I was on the bed and she'd gone all floppy in my arms. She let me pull her undies aside a white slope a raw pink gash a little medallion of hair. I have been a good house cook Jade I said surely you know that.

She grabbed my head and pushed it down when I came up for air her eyes were closed I took that as a sign. I entered her warm and slippery I was the boss her master. I looked down at her clutching the bedhead the sinews in her arms all stretched along the bone the veins in her neck sticking out when she lifted her chin to squeal. I spasmed on her belly. She held me then let me go. I laid down gazing for a long time at her body the creamy buttery slope of her flank the vivid white where the bikini had been.

We didn't stir till after lunch when we heard noises in the drive and someone arriving downstairs. When I went back to her room it was early evening she was on the bed now watching a movie on her laptop I stood at the door looking in. You will speak to your father won't you Jade I said and see what my position is? I hope to be running my own restaurant soon as you know I don't have a lot of time. Go away she said you're an idiot I don't want you here go away and cook something if you're a cook you are a cook aren't you?

After that I went upstairs to the attic and lay on the bare bed thinking. Feed her what she wants I said don't stop serving now. See how low you can go. The square of sky in the window went dark I hadn't cried for a while so I guess it was probably time. Then I went downstairs to cook.

A hot afternoon the pig long gone the last cut the trotters

honey-roasted and I'm standing on a milk crate looking off into the distance with I don't mind saying a fair bit of pride at my vegie patch all tall and lush and green splashed with marigolds and violets and nasturtiums and beyond that further down the garden my coops and runs one beside the other chickens turkeys geese pheasants pigeons quails and beyond that again grazing on the lawn at the end of its rope the ewe I brought back from Wallan. Four and a half months pregnant seventy dollars cash. I talked him down from eighty. I have used her milk already to make the cheese her lamb I'll stuff with it flavoured with black truffle shavings slow-roasted and served in its juices. Don't move your head the Mistress says.

There is a big meal coming the Master is entertaining a businessman from Hong Kong a very important businessman he says a very important meeting I must serve only the best. For entrée stuffed squab with a balsamic dressing for mains the lamb stuffed with its dead mother's cheese and for dessert poached pears *Belle Hélène* with vanilla ice-cream and candied violets. The days are busy it doesn't stop feeding the Mistress the Master fretting over the big meal delivering food to Jade in her room doing it with her there in the attic the bathroom wherever whatever she wants. All this I'm thinking standing there in the sun. The Mistress has her blue smock on her palette in one hand her brush in the other craning her head sometimes this way sometimes that squinting against the light. Sometimes she can't help herself she speaks to me in

French. *Très bien* she says when I manage despite the gazing and thinking to stay as still as a post or *immobile s'il te plaît* when I don't.

I stand like that for more than an hour listening to her instructions all the while gazing at my handiwork planning in my mind in intricate detail the forthcoming businessman's meal. Delicious! he will say absolutely delicious but where do you get your produce? I grow everything here on the property I will say. He nods his head impressed and turns to the Master and asks might he perhaps be persuaded to let this young man go? The Master laughs. But says the businessman I would very much like to give this young man the opportunity of running his own restaurant in Hong Kong money no object he says. The Master laughs even louder. Do you really think I would let him go he says I will never let him go I have plans for this young man a restaurant in Melbourne that will be famous throughout the world his name synonymous with Escoffier Thuillier Ducasse and Pic.

The sun was going down behind the trees the evening muggy a rumble of thunder in the distance all right said the Mistress now if you don't mind. I didn't muck around I knew what I had to do I unzipped my trousers and dropped them then started unbuttoning my jacket. Slowly slowly she said. It didn't feel bad out there in the warm evening air looking with my chin up off into the distance towards my garden and menagerie down there past the trees. The Mistress didn't know they hadn't paid their bills and anyway why should she care? Laissez-faire they call it. Haughty. Standing there thinking that I couldn't help lifting my chin a bit more like I imagined haughty to be. Good good that's good said the Mistress she liked my chin like that.

The rain was getting closer the air was heavy with it after a while she started packing up her easel and paints. *Merci beaucoup* she said. She will finish me off tomorrow. I dressed and bowed and made my way back through the garden to the house. The ewe was bleating the birds cooing and clucking they knew the rain was coming too. Back in my room I wrote out my recipes making lists of ingredients a chart of prep time and for each dish a few rough sketches of my plates. This was my last chance it had to be perfect. My lamb a tiny cube of white loin meat a smear of stuffing a drizzle of *jus* pale and tinted a slight rose colour from the blood. I heard the Mistress in the hallway the bathroom door opening the shower going on I waited a while then did the right thing pretending I was going to the toilet. The room was full of steam she gave a little gasp. Excuse me I'm sorry I said.

I felt around up the back of my sock drawer and took out the jar with my truffle in it I had not looked at it let alone smelt it for months. I unscrewed the jar but I didn't bring it to my nose no I just let the aroma come to me an aroma of grass and earth and of late afternoons in the grounds of the manor the groundskeeper in his beret and breeches his stick striding out before him his spaniel at his side behind him in the cellar a *broutart* lamb hanging six days the dark meat giving off its irresistible odour walking down past the daffodils and crocuses to the grove of ilex oaks where now the spaniel's ears are up.

I have overfed her I should have known. Wednesday a whole bottle of pinot and half a packet of salt. She lay in her pen all day panting her eyes glassy and fixed. Next morning I tried to stand her up but her legs kept going out from under her. There was mud all over her udders. Only two days to the dinner and I could feel the Master watching from the house.

That afternoon she died. I cut her open the lamb inside long dead and putrid-smelling I dug a hole and buried them both down the back. I went to my room and rifled through my recipes stuffed goose legs with a chestnut custard and garlic *purée* quails roasted in vine leaves larded with bacon and garnished with watercress and lemon a swan from the park skinned and roasted the hide sewn back on the neck wired to a natural curve the whole thing brought in on a mirror-board so it looks like it's swimming on a lake.

Then that evening in the rain the strangest thing I ever saw I still can't believe it now. I was standing near the kitchen door shaking out the tablecloth when I saw the Master running down past the gazebo waving his arms and shouting. One by one he opened up all my coops and pens and shooed out all the birds them squawking and flapping and running off in all directions. The Mistress came out to watch. Fuck off fuck off I could hear him saying fuck off out of here all of you!

But you will ask him? I said. I was standing at the attic window looking down onto the yard. Chickens pheasants quails still wandering around down there in the morning air a white duck in the black water at the deep end of the pool shaking the drops from its wings. Sure she said sprawled naked on the bed a glass of pinot in her hand. The light was beautiful up there in my old attic room. In my left pocket the business card I had made my name and number on it and the word Chef written above. A food motif border. I was playing with it while I spoke. In my right pocket the old red tea-towel rolled up tight. My position here has become very uncertain Jade I said. She popped one of my little salt-encrusted honeydew melon balls into her mouth. I have served you all faithfully I have never refused an order or cooked to anything but the highest standards I have done everything you have ever asked even things I shouldn't. I want you to tell your father I want you to say it like this that you think the cook has earned his reward. You should let him go. Help him set up his own restaurant down by the docks. It's what I deserve Jade I've earned it. You said you would. You're his favourite I know you can help.

Jade looked at me like I was an alien which funny I

suppose I was. Shut up she said. But you will ask him? I said. Sure she said. I looked at her lying there like that like all the world was hers. Come on she said. I lay down beside her. The shaft of sunlight moved down the wall and slid across her thigh. What about the chocolate? she said.

Quiet all quiet just quiet enough kids what can you do? She must be seeing that boy I say she must be staying with him. I didn't know she had a boy says the Mistress. She'll come back when she's hungry says the Master. He's got other things on his mind. I tell him don't worry I've got a good meal planned I will do something nice for sure.

In the garden a humid day after the rain I spent a while going through the rows killing the thrip. The air was heady. I had good tomatoes carrots leeks lettuce bright young baby beans. Perfect little Dutch cream potatoes. I'd worked out my menu and was happy with it. I'll carve the meat at table and dress and garnish it there. Serve the sides with one hand hidden. Let the Master taste the wine. I will explain politely each element of each dish my philosophy of freshness and youth. We must slaughter and pick our ingredients young the younger the better I will say. It is only young living things that have what the French call the *élan vital* in them the living force. Milk lamb unborn veal *poussin* squab juvenile vegetables microherbs. I will explain how in Insouciance all these young things will be served fresher than fresh-shucked oysters. You will hear the lamb bleating on the way to the slaughter.

My Master's guest will be impressed by all this he will talk about me after but most impressed of all will be the Master himself. All that time in my house he'll think right there under my nose. Give that kid a break he'll say he's more than just a cook.

Dear Hunter thanks for your visit what can I say it blew me away you coming to see me like that Huntsman I said no way when they told me it can't be him there's no way it can be him. I was so jumped up with all that stuff I wanted to say they had to give me something after. Write it down they said. They always want you to write it down.

You should have stayed. I could have shown you around the garden that's where I'm really happy you remember the garden at Cook School those little tomatoes like jewels Fabian put them in our hands the smell of oxygen and warm earth? They give me an hour in the afternoons. Nothing if it rains. It took me a while to convince them I just wanted to help things grow. The sights and smells Hunna the sights and smells! Summer now and everything's jumping up out of the ground beans French and winged mixed lettuce baby spinach heritage carrots garlic shallots tomatoes four different kinds. I get computer access too books on request I'm always storing up new recipes working out new things. Mum's come in a few times but not my sister Tash. Mum didn't stay long either. She's not well her breathing heavy every breath a drama she gets fatter by the day. She spends most days watching telly now we are nothing without telly. Soon she'll die and I'll get half the house that might be enough to get me started. Oh Hunter I'm itching to get back to it you don't know how much it hurts but they won't let me in the kitchen because of the knives. Instead I have to lie in bed and stare at the ceiling and dream up a kitchen all kinds of dishes I wish I could have shown you the good sketches I stick on my wall.

I stayed two months after you left Head Chef never did come back. Then there I was stringing beans one day when a car pulled up outside. Get in says the driver and he takes me to this big house in a leafy street a big gate a fountain a pond the driveway a yellow brick road.

I'm their cook. They give me a room and a kitchen you should have seen it you could have run ten staff in there fixed a hundred covers a night. Ian's a stock market player Deidre fifty-odd filling her days. I got to like her in the end. I called him Master her Mistress. Two daughters sixteen and twenty-three. A Miele blender a Cusipro food mill a Thermomix a Magic Freeze liquid nitrogen a blowtorch a dehydrator vacuum packer immersion circulator you name it two services a day breakfast and dinner everything whatever I wanted on account from my suppliers. Gourmet meats gourmet fruit and veg gourmet provedore local and imported whatever I wanted Tuscany porcini Baltic caviar you name it. I ask the butcher for a loin of Flinders Island lamb the flesh salty from the sea air and bang next day I'd have it. The little Indian guy at the produce store he once got me a duck from Nantes! I only ever had to click my fingers Hunter you see how the slave becomes master?

A couple of months at that place and I had become part of the furniture living up there in my little room with all my things looking down at the daughters lounging by the pool. They didn't mind they liked a bit of boy-blood the older one with her nose up the other one young just finishing school ready for the big adventure. I always made sure I let the family see me running here and there wearing my uniform getting into my hatchback yes they gave me a car to drive down to the shops. Carrying the bags back inside making a big noise. There's our cook they'd say he's working for us there's our boy. And with my back bent eyes straight I'd say yes that's right I am. Pleasing people Hunter it's a full-time occupation you can run yourself ragged with it.

Over a year at that house and one night I saw Head Chef sitting on the couch talking to the Master. It took me a while to figure it out. The Master was Head Chef's investor and when it all went to shit and believe me Hunna it did the Master said what can you give me? Head Chef said nothing I've got nothing I started with nothing now I've got nothing again. My wife wants a cook says Ian have you got someone you could give me? I'll carry your debts till you trade yourself out and no-one needs to know. Sure says Head Chef. Fixed.

Now Head Chef's back begging but this time the Master says no. He can't pay the bills. Everything's on account Hunter nothing's been paid for do you understand what I'm saying? Everyone owes everyone! The Master owes Ray the butcher but Ray the butcher owes people too so he goes to the bank and asks for a loan and the bank says sure Ray no problem because they've borrowed from another bank and that bank's borrowed from somewhere else and in his room late at night in front of his computer the Master or someone like him is betting on that bank not being able to pay. You can hear the axle creaking Hunter the bolts shearing the train picking up speed the sound of twenty pheasants frying in goose fat will not drown it out.

She was home that day from school. A bowl of chicken soup. She'd given me the look earlier it had gotten under my skin now I couldn't get it out like an itch you can't scratch. I fucked her in her room on the bed on the floor in the attic anywhere all the time doing my duty dinner on the table every evening at seven. So where's my ticket out? She's your ticket out I said Daddy's little girl find your way to the father through the daughter. I was in her ear every chance I got. You will tell your dad what a good job I'm doing? I've told you about my restaurant haven't I? Shut up and put your head down there.

We lay there for a long time that morning in the attic the spurt of blood when I did it came right out and hit the wall. I tried to stop it but it kept on glooping so I scrunched a sheet up and held it there her eyes rolling back in her head. I checked the corridor and dragged her into the upstairs bathroom and laid her down in the bath. I stood for a while watching her fade thinking about the cuts and how exactly I would do it. First off with the head then the legs stabbing and slicing through the tendons put the breast aside go back to the neck the scrag end off hack through the saddle the middle neck off the best end the shoulder back to the saddle cut it in half two loins then trim the ribs. It took me an hour then another hour to clean up. I stuffed all the bits into the big esky and put it in the boot. Late that afternoon I drove to Ray's and sorted it into tubs.

They never missed her. Two days to the big dinner and it's like oh she's run away with her boyfriend but she'll come back when she's hungry. A Hong Kong businessman fat fleshy face the Mistress out to dinner with friends did I tell you she wants to take me to France yes well that's another story. Roast haunch of venison stuffed with truffle wrapped in caul fat served with truffled mash roasted baby carrots and steamed baby green beans. I called her venison because she looked like a long-legged little deer. I was at it all day in the kitchen early doing my neck bone stock for a *jus* the bones simmered four hours the liquid strained and reduced then at the last minute a bit of blood and truffle shavings added. A very rich *jus* you'd need just a drizzle good rich colour on the plate. The boned haunch browned and roasted twenty minutes on medium-high the meat inside still pink one *tranche* per plate a drizzle of *jus* a *quenelle* of truffled mash three carrots six beans each. For entrée poached brains sautéed in butter an *amuse-bouche* of crispy skin and candied orange for dessert home-churned vanilla ice-cream with a raspberry *coulis*. By early afternoon I had it all under control.

Surprise is everything in cooking show them the left then hit them with the right at El Bulli a spinach leaf tastes like an oyster at The Fat Duck they do a poached egg made of swede. When the Master and his guest cut and tasted the venison they said it reminded them more of chicken or pork. I explained with my hands clasped behind my back that it was indeed deer but young deer that had not been allowed to roam and graze. It had been milk-fed and mollycoddled I said and this was why the flesh was so pale and delicate. I explained how the word venison came from the Latin to hunt but that this beast on the contrary had come willingly to the knife. They smiled and nodded at that the Master especially impressed. Not everyone understands the idea of provenance.

There were compliments all round when I came back out to clear the dishes the Hong Kong businessman started clapping short sharp claps with a fixed grin on his face. I did some bowing and took the plates back to the kitchen. I gave them plenty of time before I brought in the desserts slipping my business card into the pocket of the jacket hanging on the back of the businessman's chair. The Master didn't notice. Aside from eating his daughter he'd already drunk too much wine which together must have made for a heady experience. Thank you Chef you may go he said making sure his guest knew who was boss. I made sure he knew who was servant bowing low again.

I didn't come out of my kitchen again until I heard the goodbyes. I had only just started clearing the dessert dishes when the Master came back in. The cat that ate the cream. Yes he said with a little air punch you've saved me son I've clinched it get a glass have a drink I have never seen such a happy face. That my son was a deal-making meal! I did what he told me soon I wouldn't but not yet. He clinked his glass against mine. This is a tough business he said but I can tell you now as soon as that main course hit the table I knew I'd pulled this one off. Compliments to the chef he said compliments to the chef. People look ridiculous when they're ridiculously happy. The Master took the leftover bottle of wine off the table and with it in one hand and his glass in the other he made his way upstairs.

How alone was I then Hunter cleaning up the last of that mess? I'd done all I could. The venison scraps I fed to the dog the little mutt loved them why wouldn't it? The rest of her would stay in the tubs in the coolroom at Ray's I thought there was a fair chance he'd get pinned. Yes Your Honour I would say he often spoke of the daughters in a sexual way and expressed resentment at the monies owed. You can only try. I put the last load of dishes in and threw my uniform in the wash. I went upstairs to pack. That was the best meal I ever served Hunter you have absolutely no idea. Didn't we sit up on the hill there and dream of meals like that?

There was a shivering little bundle of heat inside me something warm and ecstatic when I packed up the Prius said goodbye to that suburb and drove. Moonlight on the leaves and a kind of burning behind my eyes and a heart hammering hard at my ribs. It was a surprise all right when I got there I didn't know how I just drove. The place all overgrown and abandoned the vegie garden gone to seed the fruit trees unpruned a stench of rancid water from the tanks. Kids had broken into the house. I drove right down to the shed but Terry wasn't there he was up in the Valley with you of course bouncing the next generation on his knee.

I poked around the shed for a bit the makeshift living quarters up the back the rusty patch of gravel where he used to slaughter the lambs. I walked the track to the top of the hill a big moon and a big wash of moonlight all round. I took out my phone and checked to see if the businessman had rung but there was nothing there except an old unopened message from her. *Upstairs bring chocolate too* it said. I saw lights in the distance way out over on the road two cars coming stealthy and silent. They turned into the drive. A cop got out with a torch. The other car drove around the track towards the shed where the pink Prius was parked like a beacon.

Did I tell you about the factories back home mucking around after school climbing through the hole in the fence cutting across the open ground to the steel ladder on the side wall and climbing up? An industrial estate the death smell coming off it and an awful deadly silence. You could see everything from up there Hunter the grid of buildings about twenty in all then the houses the roads and way back beyond that sitting squat in the haze on the flat horizon jewels glinting off the tallest tower and a low rumble like from under the earth the city.

By the time I left that place there was only one factory still going and I remember one late afternoon up there hearing the whistle blow. The machinery went quiet and the workers started filing out. Asian every one of them even from that distance I could see. They moved like ants filing out of their nest into the carpark the motors starting up the indicators coming on the cars making tracks home. The last one out was an Anglo in a suit jangling his keys I followed his car down the street and after that in my imagination through all the streets and arterial roads towards the city. But the supervisor didn't get to the centre Hunter that's what I saw in my mind's eye. Do you get it? Even he was not high enough for that. He would make it to a fringe suburb or the outer edge of an inner suburb but he wouldn't reach the middle. Fat chance of staying there even if he did. The city gates are closed to us we are dwellers on the fringes neither out nor in. If I lose a star I'll kill myself said Loiseau. And he did.

It's not so bad here. Blokes and bunks and bad dinners at long tables with blunt knives and forks. Just like Cook School really. I snaffle the cutlery when I can but they're onto me now. I'd forgotten how good it felt hurting yourself better that's for sure than letting others hurt you they never do it right. Chef's hands Hunter scars and burns hands forged in the heat of service. I'm in solitary under watch. There's a little window in my door to look through hello yes sir I'm still here still dreaming of slow-braised pig cheek with celeriac cream and mushrooms veal tongue with baby cuttlefish and chestnuts. That was the best venison ever you've never tasted anything like it what else was I supposed to do?

The days pass quietly the bed the four walls the door with the little window. I let myself drift to what might have been and might still be. The biggest event on the culinary calendar and only a week to opening. The builders have moved out the painters have moved in the walls all bones and alabasters and creams. The equipment imported the best you can get everybody's jealous the white chairs and tables go in. Opening night I'm like the eye of the storm soap stars footballers celebrity chefs maybe even a politician. Silk suits and cocktail dresses diamonds Rolex watches my god they look so tanned and clean. I work the room they all want my ear or to shake my hand or touch my shoulder. We start with seared salmon and caviar *amuse-bouches* and follow that with a microslice of beef tenderloin with horseradish and a watercress garnish then the *coup de grâce*. The waiters all in white move to the four corners of the room music plays and I enter from the kitchen leading a lamb on a rope. I'm wearing my whites the lamb has been shampooed the rope is white I lead it to a low white marble block standing in a white circle in the centre of the white room. I take out my slaughtering knife worn from sharpening the old wooden handle very smooth. I let it glint in the downlights. Everyone's watching. They've heard there'll be some theatre.

I lift the lamb with my arms under its belly up onto the block lay it down put my knee on it and run the blade across its neck. Some of the women gasp. There's a raw pink gash there in the throat of the lamb until the blood starts to fill it up. Then the music goes up a notch because now the real theatre starts.

All that white and now the red in drips and spurts at first then rivers and pools pouring down over the white marble block onto the white marble floor. Everyone starts applauding no-one's upset they've paid good money why would they be? The women are blushing and quivering the men are nodding yes that's how it's done. I let the lamb bleed for a while the red pool spreading across the floor then I change knives and start butchering focussed and fast. Everyone is swooning no-one could have imagined a chef having skills like this. The red has taken over the block the floor my white uniform my arms there's even some on my chin. I pull the hide up over the animal's head chop it and the tail off and get to work on the carcass.

The music swells we hear a whirring sound and at one end of my restaurant what the customers thought was a wall starts to rise. It is a roller blind behind it the greenhouse where my Sous and Commis Chefs with wicker baskets on their arms are picking green beans from a trellis pulling up potatoes plucking microherbs and flowers. There is a loud ooh from the crowd. The chefs carry their baskets back into the kitchen and now there is activity in the main dining room too.

Two waiters are taking away the hide and offal while two others bring in a charcoal brazier and light it. I have worked the lamb quickly down to the loin and the loin down into cutlets one waiter fans the brazier the other brings me a side towel to wipe the blood from my hands. My chefs wheel in a bench from the kitchen tailor-made hot plates drawers banks a flat surface at one end for my pass. I throw my cutlets no hanging no ageing onto the hot brazier the odour fills the room while the waiters mop the blood from the floor and before the astonished eyes of my customers the vegies are prepped and cooked. On a big rectangular plate two cutlets angled bone up a side of young *haricots* and baby carrots a *quenelle* of truffled mash a drizzle of rosemary and red wine *jus* a garnish of watercress and baby kale and on the blank white space remaining my name Zac stencilled in dried truffle powder.

Before the customers know what is happening each of

these plates has been whisked from the pass by my waiters and laid in front of them on the tables. People start applauding the clapping resounds around the room. The bench is rolled back the rest of the floor and marble slab is cleaned and everything goes quiet while my guests eat. You can feel the swoon in the room the men hard the women wet they can't believe what they are eating they'd heard the rumours but nothing had prepared them for this. I go back to the kitchen and change my uniform all crisp and white again the restaurant too the white blind lowered everything returned to white.

When I wander out before dessert there is a standing ovation. It's not like I don't deserve it. I'll be all over the papers tomorrow and the magazines after that. The papers the magazines the telly then all over the net. Good afternoon viewers today I'm doing quail. We never stop working. Little steps little steps. Oh Hunter. How are you and Rose? And the kids I don't know their names.

ACKNOWLEDGMENTS

Although *The Cook* is a work of fiction, I have used a number of resources to help construct the gastronomic world of the book.

For insights into the restaurant kitchen and the life of the professional chef: Anthony Bourdain: *Kitchen Confidential* (Harper, 2000), Marco Pierre White: *The Devil in the Kitchen* (Orion, 2006) and Bill Burford: *Heat* (Knopf, 2006). For ingredients, dishes and ideas for dishes: *The Concise Larousse Gastronomique* (Hamlyn, 1998), Stephanie Alexander: *The Kitchen Companion* (Penguin, 1996), Charles Sinclair: *The Dictionary of Food* (A&C Black, 1998) and *Coco* (Phaidon, 2009). I have also drawn inspiration from (and in some instances directly on the menu items of) the websites of the following restaurants: *El Bulli*, *The Fat Duck*, *Vue de Monde*, *Cumulus Inc* and *Quay*. For its historical insights I have referred a number of times to Alexis Soyer's *Pantropheon*, published as *Food, Cookery and Dining in Ancient Times* by Dover (2004). For the references to food commodities trading I have used Paul Roberts: *The End of Food* (Bloomsbury, 2008). Special thanks to Mark Briggs for letting me into his kitchen.

The epigraph is from Robert Walser, *Jakob Von Gunten* (New York Review Books, 1999), translated by Christopher Middleton.

Thanks to my agent, Melanie Ostell, for getting in touch when she did and for all her wisdom and guidance since. Thanks to my editor at Text, Michael Heyward, for his great passion and razor-sharp eye. Special thanks to Kevin Pearson at Black Pepper for being the first to give me a home and for his valued and ongoing support. Thanks as always to my friend, Paul Adkin (Arch), to whom more than can be said here is owed, and above all thanks to Susie and Grace, for living with it (and me) for so long.

This project was supported by the Victorian Government through Arts Victoria.